DARK LANE ANTHOLOGY

Volume 1

"DARK LANE ANTHOLOGY VOLUME 1"

EDITED BY

TIM JEFFREYS

ISBN: 978-1-326-21865-2

Cover artwork by David Whitlam
www.davidwhitlam.com

Cover design by Martin Greaves.
Interior artwork by Vikki Yeates, Sally Barnett,
and Martin Greaves.

Contents

Introduction

Martin Greaves

Hello, and welcome to the first *Dark Lane Anthology*. The first Quarterly Collaborative was launched in 2010 in a response to the avalanche of digital publishing available specifically online. We happy few, we band of brothers decided to re-invent the wheel in some small way, to produce a quarterly pamphlet of stories, poems and art in a lovely package of A5 black and white printed paper. No scrolling, no pop-ups, just the crisp turning of the leaves to discover what lay beyond the next page.

In producing this three-monthly hard copy we did not wish to appear like old fuddy-duddies railing against that there new technology of t'interweb. We aren't Luddites seeking to smash the Spinning Jenny or revolting peasants hurling our clogs at the Industrial Revolution. We do not wish to appear like General Custer at Little Bighorn, fending off the marauding hordes of Lakota and Arapaho, not least because Custer was an Indian killer and probably deserved his ghastly fate, though it is noteworthy that even he had time to marvel at his cavalry riding freely through vast meadows of wild flowers, which suggests he did at least have some poetry in his black heart. We aren't Leonidas and his three hundred standing defiantly at the Hot Gates, for if anything the tidal wave of digital technology that we are responding to is most definitely the future, whereas the multitudes of Xerxes' vast army was most definitely anchored in the pagan past. Why am I suddenly using these military metaphors? I have no idea dear reader, but stay with me.

The overriding reason for investing our hard earned into producing a quarterly issue of imaginative fiction is very simply *love*. We just adore the printed page. We revel in its tactile nature, we love to caress the covers of a book, to gaze at its artwork and stroke the pages flat as we turn them. It's still there, this love of the printed object, the human attraction to the written page began way before Gutenberg in 1440. Maybe it dawned with the beautiful clay Cuneiform tablets from the 4th millennium BC, and was perhaps best expressed in the illuminated manuscripts of the 7th century, where the creation of the book as *objet d'art* perhaps reached its zenith. But to hold a book in the hand brings marvellous delights that the backlit computer screen just cannot deliver.

Imagine the Magna Carta being typed up on a laptop at Runnymede and sent out as an attachment. Think of the Declaration of Independence as an email. It just doesn't work does it? Some things are just meant to be put down on paper with beautiful, glorious ink, that arterial lifeblood of the human cultural being. You cannot digitally replicate the thrill of rummaging through a cardboard box on a market stall and finding a dog-eared copy of the wonderful Ray Bradbury novel *Fahrenheit 451*, bearing the famous Ballantine cover by Joseph Mugnaini. No siree, not in our opinion!

This anthology contains a selection of the best work submitted by our stable of contributors and we sincerely hope you enjoy some, most or (ideally) all of it! The writing in here was produced not so much for profit, but was created between washing up, feeding the dog, changing nappies, clocking in and clocking out, running for a bus, grocery shopping and all of the other mundane tasks that overtake our collective lives. The stories, poems and pictures reproduced between these covers (indeed, the covers themselves!) were brought into existence by that innate human urge to create something tangible in order to inform, educate or entertain. We simply wish to tell a story, to draw an image, to fashion an item of minimalist beauty, designed to be held, admired and perhaps passed on. It's an attempt to scratch that itch of desire that burns inside most all of us. How wonderful it would be to think that copies of the *Dark Lane Anthology* itself might one day be discovered in a cardboard box or a second hand bookstore and poured over by a fellow traveller with a fondness for the printed page. It might only be a modest fantasy, but it has poetry in its heart.

MARTIN GREAVES

My approach to editing this anthology, as with the Dark Lane magazine itself, was an attempt to sidestep the idea of 'genre'. *Genre* is a notion that bogs a lot of storytellers down. As a writer myself of what many people might refer to as horror stories (quite rightly in most cases I admit), I've never actually considered myself a horror writer. I'm not even much of a horror fan, if I'm honest. I just write what comes out.

My favourite 'horror' stories were actually written by authors not linked to the genre at all. Stories like Nobakov's 'Wingstroke', 'House of Flowers' by Trueman Capote, or 'The Rocking Horse Winner' by DH Lawrence. I'm not trying to be snobbish, here, or show off my reading list. My point is that even people who say they don't read genre fiction have probably read stories such as they ones mentioned above, which to my mind definitely could be considered horror stories. By the same token, I think that considering oneself a horror writer can be self-defeating. *I'm a horror writer so I must write about zombies.* Well, possibly. But not necessarily. Let's just do away with the idea of genre, shall we, for a moment?

Many of the writers and artists featured here initially came to my attention when they submitted to our humble little magazine, connected with my very contrary tastes, and were published with no reward other than that of seeing their work in print. Vikki Yeates, Andrew MacKenzie, Sally Barnett, Prabu Lazarus, and George Cormack – whether they care to acknowledge it or not – are considered by us to be our own little discoveries. Other writers featured here responded to our anthology call. Either way, being able to 'discover' a writer or an artist and share their work with a wider public – in some small or large way (who knows?) - is a wonderful thing. I wanted this to be a book of surprises, my favourite kind of anthology, where the reader turns the page not knowing what to expect from each new story. Genre anthologies have their place, but with this one we wanted to do something different. We asked for 'weird tales' but our definition of 'weird' is fairly broad, as you will see. On a final note, for anyone wondering why I've got two of my own stories in this anthology, aswell as one joint contribution with Mr Greaves, it was mainly to show off the fantastic artwork that originally accompanied them in the magazine, rather than an attempt to monopolise this book with my own work. Also, due to the international backgrounds of the contributors, I have left the stories in their native version of English. Spelling will differ from UK to US/Australian English from story to story, as you will see.

TIM JEFFREYS

The Man Dogs Hated

James Everington

YOU COULD ALWAYS tell when he was out walking in the neighbourhood, because you'd hear the dogs barking all along his route. He walked most evenings, that was one of the things about him. I'd be sitting having a glass of wine with Deborah on the patio—the sun would just be sinking and the evening would have that clear, golden quality to it. And then the peace would be broken by barking, or even howling, as *he* passed a dog-owner's house somewhere—it made you shiver, a bit, to hear that wolf-like howling across the English summer.

Deborah would look at me like she expected me to *do* something, but I'd just gesture her inside. She didn't understand it wasn't for me to act unilaterally; things don't work like that here.

What was worse was when he passed a dog in the street. I saw it happen a few times. He'd just be standing there, whilst the dog-walker tried to drag their mutt away. And the dog would be snarling and slobbering and straining on its lead to *get* to him. They weren't scared of him, it seemed more like intrinsic hatred. Even the most placid of pets, even old Bob's blind-dog, would go feral at the sight of him—the smell of him maybe. You know when dogs bare their teeth and you realise how *animal* they are? Not cuddly pets at all but beasts.

I'm not a dog person, myself.

And *he* just stood there and the odd thing was he looked at them with such affection, almost simple-looking—a man who loved dogs. They wanted to tear his throat out and he just grinned like a fool in love. Maybe he was simple? It would explain a lot. But I never forget that look in his eyes. That look was why I didn't believe the stories that he killed dogs, poisoned pets. Not *those* stories, no. And events proved me right on that one.

It makes me wonder if some of the other stories about him weren't falsehoods too: him being near that playground; the strange noises from his house at night; him just standing staring at people through shop windows like he didn't realise they could see him too. Not that it makes much difference what was true and what wasn't. He *was* odd, no question, so we would have done the same as we did regardless of the specifics. We were all agreed on *that*. You can't be too careful, in a neighbourhood like this one.

I've lived here for close to twenty years now; I still remember when we first arrived, Deborah and I, and how it immediately felt like *home*. Not our new house, not being married, but the place itself, the neighbourhood.

Felt like the place I'd been aiming for all my life, the place that finally made sense of all those late nights in the office, all that schmoozing with bosses I hated. The broad streets were lined with trees—old trees, as old as the houses perhaps. Newly washed cars glinting in the sun on long, curved drives. Every house set back from the road by a large and immaculate front lawn. I remember my father saying once that front lawns were pointless; they couldn't be used, he said, they were only for show, only for other people. I thought, *exactly*. I didn't want to live in the kind of street my father had lived in.

I felt like I'd arrived.

I wondered at the time whether there'd be a price for living somewhere like this, for belonging here as much as I did. It was McFarlane who showed me that there was.

He lived alone, in the old Anderson house—we still called it that, despite the fact that the Mievilles had lived there in the interim. The Mievilles had arrived with three children, so we could see why they'd bought a big old house like that despite not really being able to afford it, as it later transpired. The Mievilles had been welcomed into the neighbourhood initially; we weren't prejudiced or anything. How a man makes his money is his own business. And we were glad someone was going to do up the old Anderson place, which was an eyesore and was starting to drag down prices for the whole street. But the Mievilles didn't do it up at all, they just left it to get worse. If they couldn't afford it they shouldn't have moved in. We were friendly enough telling them that it wasn't on, at first. And there was no prejudice, as I say.

How *he* could afford the house no one knew. He certainly didn't go to work. The postman told us he received a lot of mail, cheques he thought. From where or whom we never knew. We didn't even know *how* he'd bought the house—not through Havershaw and McFarlane like everyone else does around here. So McFarlane disliked him from the off, but that isn't to say he wasn't given a fair chance.

People thought he was odd from the start, of course, but eccentric is allowed. (Think of Mrs Needham and all her damn trinkets; think of old Bob obsessively polishing his medals, though we all know he gets them from car boot sales.) And he kept to himself, you had to give him that much. Never spoke to you unless you spoke to him first, and even then you rarely got more than a goofy smile in response. If you made gestures when speaking he stared at your hands not your face. You could tell he was odd, not eccentric but *odd*, as soon as you saw him. In the same way I knew I belonged here, all those years ago, I knew he didn't. Against the trim lawns and discrete houses he looked wrong, walking around grinning, in ill matching clothes. He stood out. He mismatched.

We gave him a chance but he never... He didn't fix his garden up, didn't repair the old Anderson place. Nor did he attend neighbourhood fetes or functions. Never applied to join the golf club or the Rotary. These things take up time, I know, but sacrifices have to be made in a place like this.

And gradually the rumours started about him; I don't know how many were actually true: he'd been seen on the school playing field late at night; he spent an unusually long time in the WCs at the library; he *never* put out any rubbish for the bin men on Tuesdays.

"You'll never guess what I heard about that man today..!" Deborah would say to me, and I never asked her who she had heard her stories *from*.

I know a few of the rumours were true: how he'd taken a cake Angie Havershaw had bought round as a welcome gift and put it straight out in his garden for the birds. I could see him from my bedroom window, standing amid all the squabbling crows and pigeons. Like I say, just odd—I mean Angie can't cook for toffee we all know that, but there are some things that you just don't do.

The stories kept piling up about him; whether each specific tale was true I don't know, but the sum total of them was. He would have to leave, just like it was made clear to the Mievilles, after it became obvious.

McFarlane called, and said it was time.

Now that I think about it, despite all his oddness I think it was those damn dogs that did for him, in the end. Their constant howling across our streets, unable to get rid of their hatred.

When McFarlane made it clear we were welcome here, truly welcome here, with his clap on the back and proffered brandy in the golf club bar, it felt like an initiation, a ritual indicating a test passed. Of course, I'd heard the stories about him by then, roguish letch that he was...but like I say eccentric is allowed. I sipped the brandy and toasted him ironically. It's an easy memory to recover, because the golf club bar hasn't changed in all these years, and neither has McFarlane.

"Welcome to the neighbourhood," he said. "I do hope I'm going to get to meet your good wife at some point?" and I made a mental note to invite him round, despite the anxiety I knew Deborah always felt entertaining strangers. "So nice," he'd continued, "to have the *right* kind of people in the neighbourhood. Not like that new couple just moved in on Victoria road..." He trailed off, and let me say the rest.

They were the first, that I was involved in.

The evening we went to speak to him, the man the dogs hated, I stepped out the front door, and already a dog was barking somewhere. McFarlane's way of making people who didn't fit in leave was simplicity itself—it was meant to be just a gentlemanly chat. Business-like—and this *was* business, of a kind. We would explain that there were places for people like us, and places for people like him, and those two sets of places didn't always overlap. In his case certainly didn't. Sometimes when we spoke to people they were even half-relieved, because the situation was surely obvious to them too. Sometimes they didn't take much persuading. And if they did, well, there were other ways.

There were about ten of us that night, more than normal. I had almost not gone, but I'd remembered Deborah's scornful look every time I'd ushered her inside the shadowy house from the patio when the howling started, and I changed my mind.

Rather than knocking on his door, we decided it best to confront him when he was on one of his odd evening walks. He had no set route but we just headed towards the sound of barking. There was a sense of camaraderie on these occasions, a sense of shared purpose. But I don't mind admitting that feeling was strained that night; it was almost spooky, to be out walking at sunset and hear all those dogs howling and yapping at the sky. I felt a little nervous. I hadn't with the Mievilles, hadn't for years, but I did that night.

We saw his shadow first, stretched and black in the sunset. It moved with the same aimlessness that he did—like he owned the place. But he was surprisingly fast for that, and before we could stop him he turned up Goose Gate, which was a cul-de-sac (so why go up there?) and so we decided to wait at the bottom of the street for him to come back down. For a moment it was peaceful—he only sound the swifts screeching. Then there was a commotion—we walked up a bit to look. The newcomers at Number 20 had let their dog roam loose in their garden and it was up on its hind legs at the fence, barking like it thought it was three times bigger than it was. All we could see of him was his silhouette, which paused, like it wanted to go and befriend the thing despite the hatred in its bark. Then he slowly turned and walked back down the street, towards where we were waiting.

I'll never know whether he actually understood what we had to say to him. Oh he nodded, and said yes a few times, but his eyes still had that glazed, simple look, so who could tell? He frowned at some things, not in anger but like he didn't understand the concept at all—didn't understand housing equity or why he shouldn't talk to children. It was mostly like he heard our words but didn't grasp their import (like Angie said, maybe he *was* foreign, despite the flat accent). When he looked between us it was always a few seconds after one of us had stopped speaking and the other started.

But then his eyes lit up; he was smiling but not at us. He was looking at something behind us.

I turned to look—Mrs Douglas was slowly walking along the main street, towards the turn off to Goose Gate. She had that small yappy poodle trotting along on a lead. She called it Precious, of all things, and it had always been a noisy and cantankerous dog even before *he* had come here. It hadn't seen him yet, it was lingering behind to sniff at some piss on a lamppost; Mrs Douglas was carrying a small freezer bag with its crap in it. Better than when it had used to lie in the street, but my nose still wrinkled with distaste. I don't know who's worse, dogs or their owners.

We called out to her to stay on the opposite side of the road, so she could walk Precious past without too much uproar when it noticed *him*. But she couldn't hear us. Instead the deaf old idiot started crossing the street to try and hear what we were saying. We gestured at her to go back, and she stopped in the middle of the road in confusion.

Precious had noticed by now, and was barking and straining at its lead. The thing looked *rabid*. I thought that it must just sense that he's not right, in some way, like we did.

Get back, we said again, but she walked forward instead.

Just then two bikes came down the main street—just kids racing. Our roads are pretty quiet, so children are safe on bikes. One went one side of Mrs Douglas, one the other, and they were laughing and hollering; one reached out to tap Mrs Douglas on the shoulder as he passed—a childhood prank that made me nostalgic. It was *nothing*; but Mrs Douglas reacted like she'd been shot. She cried out, threw both her hands up in the air, staggered back a few steps. The boys went giggling off into the night; the freezer bag of dog shit flew into the air; and Precious was suddenly racing across the road snarling, lead clattering behind it. Its teeth were bared and its eyes bulged. We were all so startled we stepped back from the vicious looking thing.

I thought it was going to rip his throat out.

Of course, a small dog like that couldn't have done him much harm normally, despite how frenzied it looked. But the damn idiot bent down to it as it came, as if to pet it, as if to scoop it into a hug. He had that idiot look of affection in his eyes; his smile was wide and beatific.

Precious leapt...

The bag of shit fell back into our street and burst.

... the dog's forepaws caught him in his chest, his arms clasped the slavering dog in an embrace, and he fell backward with the impact...

Then there was one of those seconds which seemed much longer, or like you've blacked out, because everything was different afterwards.

He was lying on the pavement and Precious was stood atop him—at first I thought she was biting his face but she was just licking it. Her tail was wagging frantically and he had one hand up, just stroking her back and behind her ears. His eyes were closed.

No one knew what to do for a second—McFarlane was no bloody use—so I approached cautiously (it wasn't seemly, for him to be lying in the street as he was). I reached out for the lead, being careful not to touch the damn mutt itself, and the thing turned and growled at me with slobbering jaws. It looked at me with the hatred of dogs.

Then it turned back to him, all eager and affectionate again.

"Precious?" Mrs Douglas said weakly.

I reached out for the lead again, annoyed now. Precious turned and with no preamble, bit me in the hand.

I yelled out and stepped back; I turned to McFarlane to say something...

He was staring past me. "Look at *him*," he said.

The man had one hand against the pavement, and it was twitching. His eyes were closed and he was still smiling that smile, but his face looked grey and drained of blood. His chest was heaving up and down with slow, shuddering breaths; Precious rode up and down on it, still licking him with frantic affection. He still had one hand on the dog's back, no longer stroking but just as if to hold her in place.

"Your dog bit my bloody hand," I said to Mrs Douglas.

He died in front of us with no one moving, and then Precious stood on his chest and howled. After a few seconds there was another howl from

Number 20. And then the sound was taken up by all the dogs of our neighbourhood—barking and howling into the empty night sky.

The family who have moved into the old Anderson place seem much more acceptable—he was in finance and we know a few of the same people. They have already started doing the place up. Mind you, they should be able to afford to do so; McFarlane says they got the place for a song because no one round here wanted it. And his wife has got to know my wife, I think. It's hard to say, because Deborah is staying with McFarlane, until the papers come through and we can sell the house.

I wonder how long it's been going on.

I could afford to buy her out and stay here, and indeed have been angrily telling people that I will. That this is *my* neighbourhood as much as hers. And people at the club, or in the street, or at the Rotary fete, say yes of course you must. And then they change the subject.

I don't know why Deborah reacted like she did—who made her judge of everyone all of a sudden? And after all McFarlane and the others were there *too*. Why do they still get slaps on the back at the clubhouse? Why do they still get invites to dinner, and Angie's inedible cakes, and compliments on their lawns?

Precious had to be put down of course. Technically there was no evidence that she contributed to his death (which is still officially "unexplained") but my testimony that she bit me did for her. So I can understand why Mrs Douglas dislikes me so, but not everyone else.

I can't say I'm upset about Precious. As I say, I've never really been a dog person.

And maybe the feeling is mutual, for when I go out for a walk in the evenings (it helps me to think through my feelings about the whole Deborah thing, if I am walking) I swear that they have all started barking at *me*.

One Cup of Coffee

Matthew Lett

IT WAS NEARING midnight, the witching hour, and Daisy's Diner was about to close up for the evening. It was a dingy, non-descript little establishment that sat just off the road near the exit ramp that ran up to Route 66. The parking lot was deserted save for two cars, while inside low-hanging globes full of musty light and dead flies were being dimmed. A short-order cook in stained whites stood by his grill in the back, waiting to scrape the day's grease into its trap. Today's special had been the strawberry pie with a scoop of vanilla ice cream. A trucker favorite.

And in a booth that sat not far from the diner's main counter and cash register, was Jacob Maloney. He was sipping on a cup of coffee and wondering how he'd gotten here. He was tired, his red-rimmed eyes bleary and bloodshot from lack of sleep. The coffee was bitter, much like himself, and he was packing a loaded .38 Special inside his sports jacket; a sports jacket, off-blue in color, that he'd received from his now ex-wife last Christmas—happier times in a different life.

Still sipping on his bitter brew, watching as the lone waitress who went by the name of Maybelle (according to her plastic name-tag) rumbled by, Jacob wondered if he was doing the right thing. He wondered if there would be any pain and if this was really the correct course of action.

He wasn't here to rob the place. The .38 had only a single bullet in its chamber, and it wasn't meant for taking maybe a hundred dollars out of the cash register and then beating feet into the night. No. The bullet was meant for him and him alone. Jacob sipped his coffee, his one and only of the evening, thinking.

He wondered briefly what Charlene would have to say about it all when she found out. Found out that her no-good ex-husband had decided to blow his brains out. That Jacob Maloney, who'd lost his job and marriage due to a trumped-up charge of sexual harassment, had taken a pistol and put it into his mouth. Or maybe he had put it to his forehead and pulled the trigger, creating a nice window in the back of his skull?

Or better yet (and this is something Jacob had seen in plenty of movies) he would place the .38 under his chin, the bullet ripping through his jaw and nasal cavities, and then piercing the brain. It almost seemed more poetic that way. More final.

The silver bell above the diner's front door rang, announcing another patron. Jacob glanced at his watch—quarter till twelve—and then at the new arrival.

It was an old man of an indiscriminate age. He was dressed in a white suit and coat, and despite its many wrinkles the gentleman appeared dapper, sporting an equally white fedora with a black band atop his snowy head. In his left hand he carried nothing, but in his right was a cane yellowing with age, its silver-plated head fashioned into the form of a roaring lion.

The man looked around carefully as if expecting trouble. "Sit down anywhere you like, sugar," Maybelle called from behind the counter. She was flipping through a *Cosmopolitan* magazine, a cigarette dangling between her lips. "Be with ya' in a moment."

The old man nodded respectfully and tipped his hat. "Thank you," he said. His eyes were greenish-blue, the color of the sea at high-tide. "Get many customers this time of night?"

Maybelle shook her head. She was a black, ample woman and genial by nature, courtesy of ten years of service at Daisy's fine cuisine. "Can't say that we do, hon," she answered. "Unless you count that man sittin' by himself over there as a crowd." She chuckled at her own wit.

The man smiled politely. "I couldn't say that, now could I?" he answered. His voice had a plangent quality to it, deep and comforting. "But I'm a man who enjoys the fine gift of conversation, and I think I'll go test the waters. You think he'll mind?"

Maybelle shrugged indifferently, ash falling from the tip of her cigarette. She brushed it away. "Suit yourself, hon. I'll be over in a sec' to take your order, but mind you that the grill is closed for the night. All we have left is hot coffee and some leftover strawberry pie. Still fresh, though."

She pointed to a see-through carousel with several slices of pie rotating inside. A fly was buzzing angrily within it, bouncing off the walls of its plastic prison.

"I'll keep that in mind," the curious man in white said. Straightening his fedora, he began to walk down the center aisle of the diner passing booth after lonely booth, his lion's cane clicking off the linoleum floor after him.

Jacob's booth lay just ahead. He was watching as the old man approached his table, wondering what he wanted. He noticed the man's shoes, a little habit of his. They were scuffed and worn, probably from untold years of travelling. *Salesman*, Jacob thought, then immediately dismissed the idea. The man's hands were empty (except for an odd-looking cane); no briefcase, no pamphlets, no notebooks or folders, no nothing. So what did he want?

"Mind if I take a seat, young man?" the gentleman in white asked, stepping up beside Jacob's booth. He had a toothy smile in his mouth—no store bought dentures for sure.

Jacob regarded him for a moment. Then: "Help yourself, old-timer. Why not? Take a load off. But the coffee here is lousy. Fair warning."

The stranger slid in across from Jacob, nodding his head. His cane he laid carefully beside him. "Thank you and I'll heed your warning about the coffee given the current condition of the pie."

Jacob smiled to himself. The old man looked as if a puff of breeze could blow him away. His hands were gnarled, the knuckles bunched and swollen. Arthritis no doubt. "Have a name, do you?"

"Indeed I do, young man." The old man sat up a bit straighter with an effort, smoothing out the lapels of his suit. "My name is Lucius Van Hoof, and it's a pleasure to make your acquaintance. You'll forgive me if I don't shake hands." He held up one arthritic hand in display. "It's a burden I must bear, you understand."

Jacob waved him away. "No problem," he said. "My mother had a touch of the arthritis so I know where you're coming from. Speaking of which, where *are* you coming from? You travelling through?"

Before Lucius could answer, Maybelle came rolling up beside them like a ship listing to port. "Get you all something?" she asked. She had an order pad in hand and a stub of pencil with bite marks on it.

"I'm fine," Jacob said.

"I can warm it up for ya', sugar. No charge."

Jacob shook his head. "No thank you. One cup of coffee is more than enough."

"Suit yourself. What about you, hon?" Maybelle asked turning to Lucius. "Change your mind about that pie? Made it fresh this morning, yes sir. I can..."

"No...no," Lucius cut-in, "I don't need any pie tonight, dear lady. But I would like a cup of coffee, and make sure that it's hot. Very hot. The warmth of the cup alone will do my hands good. Thank you."

Maybelle stared at him a moment as if the old man had just ordered a slab of raw hamburger with an egg on top. Then she smiled, her teeth a pearly-white. "One hot cup of coffee," she repeated, not bothering to write it down. "For the warmth of the cup. Right?"

Not waiting for an answer, Maybelle set sail down the aisle, her thighs grinding together like tectonic plates. If the old man dressed in his ivory suit wanted a hot cup she'd get him one, no biggie. But dammit, she thought, her feet were hurting tonight and it was almost closing time. And if those two thought she was going to stand around all night and watch them jaw over cold coffee and hot cups then they were sadly mistaken. And they had better leave a tip!

"You asked if I was travelling, right, Mr...,"

"Maloney," Jacob said. "Jacob Maloney. Sorry about that, forgot my manners."

Lucius smiled, holding his crippled fingers up. "No need to apologize, Mr. Maloney, happens to the best of us. And to answer your question, yes, I am a traveler of sorts. A nomad, you might say. I'm a man who gets around from place to place and from here to there and back again."

Jacob asked, "What are you selling?" The old man's eyes were shining at him like twin jewels; not only staring *at* him, but through him as well. He felt a twinge of unease, a ripple effect down to the base of his spine.

Lucius barked out raspy laughter—*old laughter*, Jacob thought—that turned into a brief coughing fit. When he had himself under control again, he continued: "I assure you, Mr. Maloney, that I'm not a salesman or a common peddler on the street. What I have to offer I give away freely. I consider it a "gift," for want of a better term."

Jacob grunted, tearing his eyes away from those penetrating orbs of turquoise staring back at him. *A man could drown in there*, he thought distantly. *Actually drown, no matter how hard he swam*. It was a chilling image.

"Here's your coffee, hon." Maybelle had returned. She was smoking a fresh cigarette, circlets of smoke like tiny halos about her head. "Anything else?" she asked, setting the steaming cup in front of Lucius. The cup rattled on its saucer, but didn't spill.

"No, dear," Lucius said, "I think that will be quite enough for now. Thank you."

"Suit yourself. You both know we close at midnight, don't you? This ain't no twenty-four hour stop. We've got more class than that. So I'm gonna' start cleaning up now but I'll save your table for last so you all can finish your coffee. Sound good?"

"That would be—"

But Maybelle had already disappeared into the gloom of the diner, a trail of smoke in her wake. If not for the fresh cup of coffee in front of Lucius, it was as if she had never been there.

Lucius said, "It would appear our time is limited, Mr. Maloney." He had both hands wrapped around his cup, savoring the heat creeping into his swollen joints.

"What sort of gift were you talking about?" Jacob asked. He was staring into his own mug, the coffee now ice-cold. It didn't matter. In the back he could hear Maybelle's voice floating back, hollering at someone named George to mop the kitchen floor.

"It's a simple gift, Mr. Maloney," Lucius said. He was leant forward, his elbows resting on the table. "It's called freewill, and although you already have it, you're choosing not to use it. Isn't that right?"

"What the hell are you talking about, old man?"

Lucius smiled slyly at him like friends sharing an old and dark secret. "I think you know, Mr. Maloney. It's right there in the breast pocket of your jacket."

Jacob shifted uncomfortably, the weight of the pistol like a chilly hand against his heart. How could the old man have known that? Lucky guess? Maybe, but Jacob didn't think so. Somehow the old man had known about his impending suicide—had looked right through him like an open window—and was calling him on it. But how?

"I still don't what you're talking about, mister. You're not making sense and I don't have time for riddles."

Lucius sighed, a sad-like sort of smile crossing his lips. "You're right, Mr. Maloney," he said. "You don't have time because you're out of time. You're out of choices in the matter and it's time that you exercise your God-given freewill. I'm here to make it easy. Less painful, you might say."

Jacob stared at him blankly, perplexed. "Make it easy?" he repeated. Steam was rising from the old man's cup in ghostly tendrils, lost spirits in search of rest. "You better start making sense, Mr. Van Hoof."

"You still don't understand what I'm offering to you, Mr. Maloney, do you? It's really quite simple, and as I said, painless. You're not a religious man, are you?"

Jacob looked at him sharply. "Not in particularly—no. What does it matter?"

Smiling, Lucius spread his arms open in a supplicating gesture, reminding Jacob of a scarecrow lost in a sea of corn. "Then we're half-way home already, Mr. Maloney. You have no reservations or qualms about your so-called "immortal soul." Am I correct?"

Jacob shrugged. Once again he could hear Maybelle back in the kitchen. She was telling George that she was tired tonight and that her feet hurt. He was pretty certain she'd meant for *everyone* to hear it. "Never really thought about it," he answered.

Nodding in silent agreement, Lucius said, "Good, good. But I know that you're having second thoughts about your plan, aren't you? And that's why I'm here—to help you along; to make sure that there's no fuss or muss; to make certain that you get to where you're going. In other words, to be your guide into everlasting peace."

Jacob considered it a moment. The old man was obviously crazy, but his message was also compelling in a way that he couldn't explain. He felt like a moth sputtering around an open flame, unable to resist its light and warmth, but knowing all the while it was death to the touch.

But isn't that what he had been planning all along? Of course it was.

"Okay," Jacob said, his voice steady and resigned. "What's the plan? How do we do this?"

Reaching over by his side, Lucius brought his cane up, its lion's head gleaming dully in the light. He carefully tapped it with one gnarled finger. "With this," he said. "Quick, neat, and easy."

He played it slowly back and forth before Jacob's eyes; the mouth of the lion's head now opening and closing in a silent roar. "You ever read the Bible, Mr. Maloney?" Lucius asked in a silky voice. "Have a favorite scripture, do you?"

"No!" Jacob snapped. His patience was deteriorating quickly, tired of the old man's ceaseless questioning. "I told you I wasn't religious so drop it! Jeeez..."

Undeterred, Lucius went on smiling, his teeth in a prominent display of understanding and compassion. "Well I do, Mr. Maloney. I quote it often, especially in situations such as this. It goes, '*Be sober, be vigilant; because your adversary the devil, as a roaring lion, walketh about, seeking whom he may devour.*' Make sense?"

"Five minutes!" Maybelle bawled from the back. "Leave your money on the table and a tip if ya' don't mind! You all come back now!"

"Ready to go, Mr. Maloney?" Lucius asked. His smile was vulpine now; the predator upon the prey.

"More than ready," Jacob said rising from the table. He was weary and worn, rung out like an old dishrag; an empty vessel in search of fulfillment no matter how bizarre. "Let's do it."

"Excellent, then you need only to follow me."

Putting his cane under one arm, Lucius led the way with Jacob close at his heels. He was heading toward the back exit, to the gravel parking lot that lay beyond. It would be deserted save for the lurking shadows—a fitting place for a fitting end.

Lucius paused at the door, his twisted hand resting on the release bar that would lead them out. "You're quite sure about this, are you, Mr. Maloney?"

Jacob only nodded in response, too tired to answer.

"Very well then. So be it. Let freewill reign."

Lucius opened the back door and stepped out into the night.

Maybelle caught sight of her last two customers leaving. Hurrying around the counter, she also caught sight of the table they'd vacated. Empty, except for two coffee cups. No money and no tip. Bastards!

Oh, hell no they didn't! she thought furiously. *Hell no!* "George!" she cried. "Call the Sheriff! We got a couple of free-loaders out here! Sumbitches!"

A meat cleaver lay on the ceramic countertop, its blade stained with flecks of dried blood. Maybelle seized it, clenching the handle in her ham-sized fist. She knew she wouldn't use it if she didn't have to, but it would certainly make those two dead-beats think twice before pulling this shit again at another diner.

Lumbering down the aisle at the pace of a charging rhino, Maybelle hit the back door with the force of a small typhoon. She nearly fell down the wooden steps leading out into the parking lot; the door swinging open in a pane-rattling crash.

Maybelle looked to the left and the right, the meat cleaver held high above her head, scanning the makeshift lot through the twilight. It was empty—nothing but gravel and dust. A breeze stirred that caused her to shiver, the smell of sulphur in the air, but nothing else.

"Anybody out here?" she shouted. But there was no answer, and she hadn't really expected one either. The two men had simply disappeared like ghosts in a snowstorm.

But where to? Maybelle wondered. She knew there hadn't been a car in the back parking lot since nine o' clock this evening, not to mention the fact that she'd only been a few seconds behind the two bums when they made their escape and stiffed her. *So what happened to them?*

She shook her head, standing there alone in the darkness, unable to figure it out. She lowered the meat cleaver, now useless and child-like in her hand.

Damn! she thought. *And I would've showed those two boys a thing or two. Oh yeah! Stiff me will they? Stiff them! If I had two cents I'd...*

Maybelle's thoughts broke off, her mind suddenly trying to grasp a concept that seemed impossible. It was in front of her, imprinted in the dust; two sets of footprints, one right behind the other, trailing into nothing.

...trailing into eternity...

Maybelle turned to go back inside and tell George to call off the Sheriff. They wouldn't need him now, and she thought to herself—only for the briefest of seconds—if maybe those two men hadn't been sucked up into the midnight sky?

The night sighed and the diner lights went out.

Anything was possible. Anything at all.

Desert Places

Carina Bissett

They cannot scare me with their empty spaces
Between stars–on stars where no human race is.
I have it in me so much nearer home
To scare myself with my own desert places.

-- Robert Frost

CLARA OPENED HER eyes to a white sky.

A sandstone alcove covered her body with a thin sheet of promised shade, but the sun still glared overhead, creating a brilliant nimbus around the smooth overhang. Her head lolled on the rock ledge as she turned her eyes to the east, where a smudge of frosted blue bled up from the horizon into the bleached heavens.

Her swollen tongue crept out to separate her parched lips. Grains from the gritty layer of salt and sand covering her rubbed deeper into her sunburned skin as she moved.

Clara grimaced.

The salt caught on her chapped mouth, scorched her taste buds, making her retreat. She sat up, ignoring her muscles' protests and looked out at the bend where the canyon curved out of sight against a sheer cliff looming thousands of feet high.

Nothing. No movement greeted her.

Even so, she felt something watching, waiting.

All around her fallen rocks and desert plants flattened out under the harsh light as if leaving as little exposed to the brutal heat as possible. Distances deceived. Faint trails coiled out and twisted back upon themselves in a maze of ruined rock, gnarled shrubs and withered cacti. She now was aware of the labyrinth she and her husband had stumbled into. But that knowledge had a high price.

Clara glanced at her watch, one of the first things she'd shed hours earlier when rescue had still seemed an option. So alien it appeared, counting manmade minutes, ticking off time in a place where time had no meaning. The waterproof face showed that six hours had passed since she'd last seen Jay and more than eight since she'd had her last swallow of water.

Clara's eyes spasm-ed as a flood of despair washed over her, but that well had long ago run dry, even before this trip—years before. She shut her eyes and watched little curlicues of red light float against closed lids.

She drifted through the wavy patterns of violet and green that hung temptingly just at the edge of her inner eyelids and thought of that night so long ago and the many others that came afterwards—nights when despair had sent her hiding under mounds of blankets in a dark room seeking some inner revelation that meaning existed in the world, that it wasn't all in vain.

She remembered wishing she had died in place of her son. How could an infant live only two weeks and still fulfill his purpose in the world? SIDS they called it—sudden infant death syndrome, the sleeping death. He had died four years ago, but it could have easily been four months or even four days—time didn't matter and it certainly didn't heal all wounds, not hers anyway. She would never conceive again, they had told her—the doctors and specialists in their sterile priest's robes. Nathan she had called him, this boy who would never run or jump or laugh. Yes, there were many times she still wished she could join him, hold him tight to her breast in the deep, dark womb of the earth.

But now that she had no choice in the matter, now as she felt the thread of life stretch thinner and thinner, she wondered if death solved anything. She wondered how much death this isolated place had seen in its lifetime, how much death it had caused and what its own demise would mean or even if it would ever die. Do places like people die or are they forever, just transformed into another landscape in another time? Her thoughts spun, backtracked and then floated free only to be captured like a June bug on a string—glimmering with vain hope in the sunshine on its tether, searching for some meaning in a meaningless world. One thing was certain. She wasn't as ready to die as she had once thought.

Here deep within the bowels of the Grand Canyon, they had wandered unprepared for the deceit of those hard, biting layers of earth—a forbidden place where the elements had cut too deep, exposing stone and rock that was never meant to see the light of day. Clara strained to hear the whisper of water she and her husband Jay had searched for—the siren's song of the Colorado River cutting into the canyons. But the faint rustle could just as easily have been the wind echoing in the desolate depths or a ghost whispering sibilant secrets in a forgotten language.

Clara peered over the alien landscape to where the side canyon they had descended into merged with another, but Jay was still nowhere in sight. Her hand lay limply against the rainbow-colored wrap she was lying on. She stared at her skin a moment, tracing the network of blueish veins raised on the back of her hand and up her forearm, marveling at the intricate pattern exposing itself against the transparent, shrunken skin. For a moment she imagined herself as a wolf delighting in the rush of blood filling her mouth as she brought a panicked deer to the ground by its delicate neck. Then, as quickly as the image appeared, it vanished, leaving her wondering if such madness was a result of the dehydration or if it was yet another thing lurking beneath her skin, eager to see the sun at last. Clara shuddered at the thought and let her head loll back on the hard hummock of rock that served as a stony pillow before once again closing her eyes. Alone with her thoughts, she waited for the coolness of night to attempt the journey back out of the canyon to the truck—alone.

But then the feeling of something cunning watching her prompted her to snap open her eyes and spring up from her prone position—an attempt that left her dizzy with effort and clutching at the rough rock with torn fingertips. A woman sat perched on a nearby boulder crowned with the ruddy hues of a dying day. Clara blinked her eyes wearily, wondering at the odd sight.

The woman's sun-kissed skin gleamed and her hair hung down her back in a silken wave as thick and black as the darkest shadows. She was dressed simply in a loose white shirt and a trim pair of tan pants. Clara noted the handle of a blade peeking out from the top of one of the woman's worn boots and the simple necklace beaded with bits of colored stone hanging against her smooth throat. The woman's generous lips curved in a slight smile and her eyes glinted gold in the day's last light.

Clara pushed the loose strands of her own dark hair behind her ears and swallowed convulsively. "Hello?" she asked in a cracked voice.

The woman ignored her, jumped down from the boulder, turned her back and began to walk away.

"Wait," Clara pleaded. "Please wait. Don't go."

She stumbled to her feet, rocked unsteadily on fatigued legs and caught herself as a red haze flooded her vision. When her sight cleared, the strange woman was nowhere in sight. Clara slumped, sat down and buried her face in her hands.

"Of course there's no one here," she said out loud. "Who in their right mind would try to find a lost trail out here in the middle of summer?" A sobbing laugh escaped her. "Okay, I can do this."

She shook her head and walked over to the two heavy backpacks leaning against the wall of the alcove. She went through Jay's pack and removed his compact flashlight and the last orange, which she reverently sat on the rock beside her. Clara then pulled out her red sleeping bag and struggled to the top of the rocky overhang with the awkward bundle, which she unrolled and anchored with small piles of scattered stones, hoping that the bright color would reveal the location of this last camp to any rescue team she might be able to summon.

The sky began to darken quickly as the sun continued to sink. Clara peeled the orange, licking off every drop of precious liquid as she devoured the segments one by one. She remembered the smell of orange blossoms in spring and the stickiness of the fruit she'd pick in summer to squeeze each morning. She sighed wearily when the last piece was gone and tossed the rind in her packed trash bag. She picked up her makeshift walking stick and flipped on the flashlight.

"Well here we go I guess." She looked one last time in the direction Jay had gone in search of water and turned to head back out of the canyon under the coming cover of night. However, a sound or a feeling or something she couldn't quite identify brought her up short. She froze a moment, searching.

"Hello," she said in a loud voice. "Is anyone there?"

Something rustled the dry brush and Clara caught a glimpse of a coyote skulking in the shadows on the other side of the canyon. Its yellow eyes glowed as they reflected the dying sun before the animal dashed away. Clara tensed as if to bolt, shrugged it off and then began the slow process of walking out. The coyote's yipping laugh followed her under the cover of dusk. This time she didn't look back.

The night slipped down into the canyon, covering the red walls with a velvety darkness. Stars sparkled mercilessly from their lofty station in the sky. Clara concentrated on putting one foot in front of the other, leaning heavily on the stout stick. Her breath rasped harshly between cracked lips.

Sometime later the moon rose, a full pale sun. With the added light Clara could see she had somehow lost the path. She backtracked frantically. Then something dashed in front of her and froze in the bright beam of her hand held flashlight. A creature, the size of a jackrabbit, stared at her a moment with round silver eyes. Its mottled skin looked like a collection of dried leaves and its spindly, sticklike legs hugged the ground. Startled, it leapt into a collection of white boulders, which suddenly looked like the bleached remains of some slumbering giant. Clara hesitated and then laughed, a harsh, crackling sound.

"Peachy," she said to herself. "I'm losing my mind."

She plunked down on a large flat rock listening to the absence of sound.

"I know what it is," she sighed, closing her eyes to the watching night, "I'm dreaming. That's what it is. Dreaming."

Exhausted, she fell into the dark sea of dreamless sleep and drifted for a while lost in time and space—distanced from the fetters of her aching body. She wondered if this was what it felt like to be dead, this nothingness, but then the feeling of someone watching her jerked her back to her unprotected body. She lurched forward, blindly looking around for a predator ready to pounce.

The woman she'd glimpsed earlier traced her movement with glittering eyes. "Hello Clara," she said in a voice as dark as tinted glass.

"Who are you?"

The stars seemed to swirl in the deep blue velvet overhead.

"Marguerite," the woman said. A smile spread across voluptuous lips. She tossed her hair over her shoulder and jumped down from her rocky perch. "It seems you have lost your way."

"Yes." Clara's tongue darted out in an attempt to moisten her parched lips. "Do you have any water?"

Marguerite smiled. "The river is just over there."

Clara frowned. "There is no river."

"Hmmm. Walk with me."

Marguerite strolled by her, hips gently swaying. She stopped after a few feet and motioned to Clara. "Come, come. Dawn will be here soon enough."

Clara swung her legs to the ground and tested their strength as she attempted to stand. She clutched her makeshift walking cane with white knuckles and made her way to Marguerite's side. A gentle wind whispered through the canyon bringing with it the subtle smell of rain. Clara picked up her head, nostrils flaring. Her eyes leapt from horizon to horizon. Marguerite chuckled and began to walk. Clara followed gingerly at her side.

"How do you come to be here?" she asked.

"I'm writing a story," Clara said still scouring the heavens for clouds. "I was looking for a lost trail."

"Lost. Yes." Marguerite threw her head back, revealing her slim neck. The beads on her necklace danced as she laughed.

Clara shuddered and looked closer at her strange companion. Marguerite's eyes reflected the full moon. The ghostly light frosted the landscape. The desert scrub rustled.

"I was lost once," Marguerite remarked. "I first found this place while searching, just like you. Perhaps you will still find your way."

Clara frowned. "I came here with my husband. He's a photographer. Have you seen him?"

"He found the river. Others found him. He doesn't belong in this place like you and I." Marguerite tilted her head as if testing the air. "We all travel different paths, but sometimes we journey together a while, searching for similar answers." Her eyes glittered. "Interesting don't you think?"

Clara paused. "What are you talking about?"

Marguerite's full lips twisted into a wolfish smile. "Keep walking. We have a ways to go."

For hours they walked in silence. Clara slipped farther and farther from herself, from reality until she felt so light that she wondered how her feet were able to touch the ground. Dreamily, she listened to a ghostly chorus serenade the stars with a song so ethereal it seemed to pour from the lips of the canyon itself, not the coyotes she imagined it to really be. Marguerite hummed an odd harmony to the tune. Occasionally, Clara would see more of the spindly, night creatures skipping along boulders or rushing from one side of the ravine to the other. Once, she thought she caught the glimpse of a dark manshape leaping from the cliff face, but when she looked closer the figure was just a large owl, which passed by so close to her head that she was strangely curious as to how its talons had missed catching in her hair. Marguerite continued to match her lengthening strides, never passing or following, but mimicking every movement, every breath.

The scent of a desert storm strengthened, filled the night air with a wet promise. The air crackled with electricity and Clara felt her hair lift in the still air like a dark cloud hovering around her head. Without further warning the sky rent and the heavens sent a torrent of rain down upon them. Clara closed her eyes and raised her throat to the sky, letting the liquid drown her thirst. She stood there, not moving for a few minutes until the rain eased up into a thin drizzle. When she opened her eyes Marguerite grinned at her, flashing white teeth that seemed much too sharp. *My what big teeth you have*, the nursery rhyme chimed unannounced in Clara's thoughts.

Marguerite bent over and picked up a stone. She rolled it in her palm as if testing its smoothness and weight. Horrified, Clara watched as Marguerite's hand shifted, into something resembling a paw with black, curved nails. Her gold eyes gleamed and her face elongated, blurred, before finally transforming into a coyote's head. Clara felt her full weight slam back into her, pinning her to the ground as effortlessly as a butterfly caught on a collector's board. The coyote with a woman's body laughed.

"What are you thinking dear Clara?" the coyote-Marguerite asked. "Are you wondering still if you are dreaming or if you are dead or that this is all very real?" She "tsked, tsked"—teeth clacking.

Clara didn't answer, couldn't answer. She felt her legs tremble, urging her to flee. She could smell her own fear mingled with the coyote-Marguerite's delight. Clara's vision shifted and widened, allowing her to see a multitude of shadowy shapes gathered to watch their confrontation.

"I have an idea Clara," said the coyote-Marguerite. "Do you see this puddle here?"

Marguerite looked carefully at the small pool of water caught in a shallow pocket of weather worn rock. "If the stone floats you're alive. If it sinks you're dead. Yes, that should work."

The coyote-Marguerite casually tossed the rock, which landed in the middle of the puddle. Clara gasped a torn cry.

As one they gazed at the stone, its upper half protruding and its lower half hidden in the cool water. The coyote-Marguerite flashed her sharp teeth, yipping and howling as she swirled in delight under the full moon. Caught by something she couldn't understand, Clara watched helplessly as Marguerite changed back into her human image.

"It appears," she said, "you are neither alive nor dead."

Marguerite peered at Clara and her features softened a bit. She fingered the bits of stone strung around her neck. "I was once like you, trapped by fear and the uncertainty of life. And I too searched for the answer to my question." Her arm stretched out in a sweeping arc as she gestured to the canyon's savage desert. "I found my answer here and now you will wander these canyons like I have all these moons until you unravel the mysteries hidden here."

"You have brought all of your demons to this place, all of your fears and desires and pain. They walk this place with you. They stalk you. They will try to consume you. But one day, when you stop being the hunted and become the hunter, you will know you have found what you were looking for and then another tormented soul will come to take your place in this heaven, this hell. That is the price you will pay."

And then Marguerite changed yet again, a gradual metamorphosis, a stretching of time and place, until Clara found herself confronted with a mirror image—one dressed in Marguerite's clothes. Marguerite leaned over the pool, smoothing her new hair. "Yes, this will do quite nicely."

Released at last, Clara turned and fled. She ran fleetly, striking sparks against the rocks as she attempted to escape. The stars seemed to blur and the brush bowed at her passing. Marguerite's throaty laugh followed her path. Clara's ears cocked to catch the sound as that dark laugh changed into the bubbling one she had lost on the day Nathan left her. Shocked, Clara stopped and turned to look.

And saw evidence of her flight.

Her heart pounded frantically in her chest and she danced from side to side—looking not at her human footprints—but tiny, cloven deer tracks caught in the wet sand. The prints glistened briefly before being swallowed by the dark as the moon set over the canyon rim. And somewhere, hidden deep in the cracked earth, a baby cried.

Strike Three

M.R. Cosby

I LOOKED THROUGH the screen door at the man standing on our front path. He held a cardboard box at arm's length. A few paces behind stood four boys, just a bit older than me. With open mouths and slack jaws, they stared at him.

An old black van was parked on the street in front of our house. The hand-painted lettering down its flank read *Velasco & Sons, House Clearing*.

"Please, do come in," said my father. Our visitors trooped through the hall, past our open bedroom doors, to the dining room. Even though I was almost twelve, I felt the need to hide behind my father, to watch from safety as the man placed the cardboard box on the edge of our dining table. He stepped back, and his face relaxed for the first time.

"Oliver Stanton," my father said. They shook hands. "This is my daughter, Rosie. My son Christian is in his room, reading as usual." He looked at the four boys, but Velasco offered no introduction. My father bent his spidery frame towards them and tried to start a conversation. His proffered hand went unshaken. I felt my face burn as his foolish attempts at engagement came to nothing.

His knees clicked as he straightened up and shifted his attention to the box. As he unwrapped the box with gentle fingers, he made appreciative cooing noises which did not sound like him at all. I glanced over my shoulder and watched as Velasco withdrew to the hallway. Then I turned back to see the antique clock emerge from its cocoon of packaging. I was intrigued by its delicately tapered hands and its polished wooden case, as dark as coal. Unadorned on the table, it imposed itself upon the room. Instinctively, I reached out for it. My father pushed my hand away before I could do more than brush my fingertips against its veneer, but even that gentle touch made it slide across the polished surface of the table. I stared, and any amount of time could have passed.

By then, it may already have been too late for poor Christian. With a start, I thought of him alone in our bedroom, and I tugged at my father's sleeve without success. Eventually I mustered the courage to leave his side and to push through the gaggle of boys barring my way to the hall.

When I saw Velasco at our open bedroom door, my scalp prickled. I squeezed past him to get to my brother, who sat cross-legged on his bed, novel open on his lap, glasses perched at the end of his nose. They were staring at each other. Had something happened between them while they'd been apart from the rest of us? I rushed across and took Christian in my arms. At first I couldn't break his stare, and panic clutched at my throat; but as I held him tightly, he relaxed.

I looked up. The doorway was empty.

"Christian," I said. His eyes were glassy and unfocused. "Look at my face!"

Eventually he blinked and recognised me. In a sure sign of stress, he fingered the fine scar extending into his jawline (mother called it his birthmark). Then he spoke in French. Words I couldn't understand tumbled over each other. Christian was fluent in the language, yet I struggled even with the basics, despite being two years older than him. He wrestled himself away from me and pulled the bedclothes up to his chin. Just then I heard my father's voice from the street in front of the house. Reluctantly I left Christian in the dimness of our room.

Outside the heat took my breath away.

"...So you're telling me you don't have a key for the clock?" My father spoke in his loud voice. He turned and frowned at me as I approached. This allowed the man and his boys to escape, and they climbed into the van. Its engine coughed into life, and the vehicle jerked its way up the hill in a cloud of exhaust fumes.

~

That night in my dreams I heard the clock striking.

I woke in the early hours to feel my heart thumping. My first reaction was to look across to Christian's bed, and I saw the familiar shape of his figure beneath the twisted sheets. Instantly I heard movement from elsewhere in the house. This was so unusual that I listened to the sounds for some time before I dared leave the safety of my bed.

Despite having been told never to touch him while he slept, I reached out to stroke Christian's forehead as I passed. Instead of skin, I felt smooth fabric. I pulled the sheet back and found two pillows carefully positioned to fool me.

I crept into the dark hallway. Creaking floorboards telegraphed my every movement. I began to call for my mother, but the words died on my lips as I glimpsed the tiny form of my brother in the dining room. I hesitated for a moment, then it dawned on me that the sounds, which I had taken to be someone or something moving about the house, came from the clock. It ticked loudly despite the lack of a key.

The clock had been moved from the dining table to take up pride of place on the sideboard, and Christian knelt before it. Moonlight shone through the dining room windows and illuminated a pool of darkness on the floorboards in front of him. As I stared, he absent-mindedly squeezed his fingers. Blood dripped to the floor and added to the pool. I had never seen anything like it, and I froze.

The hands of the clock were almost at three. A whirring sound began as it prepared to strike the hour. Christian jumped up, then reached around to the rear of the case and plunged his hand inside. The resulting silence was complete. He withdrew his hand slowly and stepped backwards. To my surprise, he let me take his arm and guide him gently back through to our bedroom. I suppose he hadn't been fully awake. He did not even object as I shrugged off my pyjama top, wrapped his bloody hand tightly, and lay him back down in his bed.

Surprisingly, sleep came quickly for me too, and I woke late to discover Christian already up. His fingers had been neatly bandaged, and there was no sign of blood on the dining room floor.

Although he had clambered up into the loft and returned in triumph with several old keys, my father still could not bring the clock to life. He struggled and swore, and muttered under his breath, but despite his best efforts he had no luck. Eventually he stormed off to find his treasured tool kit. With nothing else to do, I studied the clock. The two winding shafts emerged from holes in its face and were of a shape I had never seen before. Absently I felt the end of one, and immediately pulled my hand away. It felt as though my finger had been sliced by something sharp, yet when I looked, there was no sign of injury.

I heard a muffled laugh from across the room, and I turned to see Christian, holding an open book as usual. I told myself he was laughing at the story instead of at my gasp of pain, yet as I later thought back to this moment, I could see how it represented the beginning of the end of our brief closeness. I could see the limit of his empathy.

He gestured for me to join him by the kitchen door. " Hey, Ro. Can you wind my watch for me?" Since the arrival of the clock, he'd been unwilling to wind his wristwatch because of his injured fingers. As I wound, something occurred to me. I suppose I must have understood all along, but until that moment I'd kept it within the deepest shadows of my mind. He had been shredding his soft and youthful skin by trying to wind the clock without a key.

That night something woke me in the early hours and, once again, the strange nocturnal ritual played itself out. By then Christian no longer felt the need to disguise the fact that he left his bed. I tried to avoid the noisiest floorboards as I made my way through to the dining room. I was no longer surprised to hear the ticking, which seemed stronger and more insistent. Once more he knelt, entranced; yet this time things were different. I was stunned by the size of the clock. It still stood on the sideboard, yet it must have been as tall as Christian. I had also never noticed the door in the wooden panel below its face. It gaped in the darkness. Machinery moved; wheels turned and gears stuttered. Cold light picked out the edges of dull metal, pocked with surface rust. I wondered at the source of that unnatural glow.

Christian stood up stiffly and crept towards the clock. As I approached, the ticking got louder, and the increasing light made the shadows within the clock even darker. The mechanism pulsed and beckoned. In a kind of panic, I rushed across the room. I grabbed his shoulder and pulled him back. He glared at me, and I was shocked by the malevolence in his young face; all trace of innocence was gone. His expression made me aware of something lurking at the back of my mind, like the dregs of a long-repressed memory. The scar on the side of his face stood out red and angry.

The ticking stopped and the light dimmed. My hand fell to my side, and I knew the danger had passed. Blood dripped from Christian's fingers on to the floor.

From then on, Christian gave the clock a wide berth. I often saw him staring at it from across the room, as though unable to look away. He looked miserable, threatened. On one occasion I followed him through to our bedroom, where he climbed back in his bed to read. As usual, I felt like an intruder in my own room. I perched awkwardly on the edge of my bed. For the first time, I dared to broach the subject with him: I wanted to ask him why the clock was coming between us, and what it meant to him, but I couldn't find the words. Instead I challenged him about its size.

"I honestly don't see how it could've got any bigger, Ro," he said from behind the pages of his book.

"But of course it has!" How could he refuse to acknowledge what to me was so obvious? "Remember—that man carried it, in a box. It's way too big for that now."

"It's a timepiece. It's made of wood and metal. It can't have grown!" He breathed out heavily to show his impatience then studied the page in his book with renewed vigour. I wasn't to be put off. A tipping point in our relationship had arrived, and there was no turning back.

"It's *obviously* bigger than it was. I don't know what's happened, and I s'pose it sounds crazy, but you can't just sit there and deny it." The anger rose within me. The sense of guilt and protectiveness I felt towards him, such a big part of my young life, was being over-ridden. "Anyway, what about getting up in the night like that? You can't tell me that's normal. All that blood on the floor, and your fingers bandaged up like that. What does mother think?"

"C'mon Ro, be reasonable..." His eyes clouded over. "You know very well I can't speak to her about it. I don't even know myself what goes on in the night–it's like a dream I can't quite remember. Maybe I'm sleepwalking or something. Either that, or *you're* doing the dreaming. Remember those nightmares you used to have? Father often tells me you're not to be trusted, you know. He doesn't even like us sharing a room." With the arch of an eyebrow, he dismissed my concerns and turned away. Something in his unflappable manner had pushed me too far.

"Come with me, then. You're so clever. Come with me and prove it hasn't changed!"

I grabbed his wrists. It worried me how easy I found it to handle him so roughly, and I'll never forget the look of resentment he gave me as his book dropped to the bedroom floor. I pulled him from the bed and dragged him into the hall. At first he struggled silently, but as I wrestled him into the dining room, he started to whimper. I was a lot bigger than he was, and his stockinged feet gained no purchase on the floorboards, so it was easy for me to drag him over to face the clock. His whimpers escalated to screams, and my father appeared. I released Christian's wrists, and then I felt myself wilt under my father's unforgiving gaze.

"Rosie, if I *ever* see you treating your brother like that again, you'll be in serious strife. We don't want to start that trouble all over again, do we?"

He turned to Christian and, as I was so used to seeing, his gaze softened. My heart broke a little.

"Christian, please go back to your room and read. I'm trying to get ready, and I can't waste time refereeing fights between you and your sister." He looked back at me and his voice took on a sharper edge. "Now,

Rosie—go and do your chores." I opened my mouth to object but his frown, and the half-formed doubts I harboured about myself, stopped me in my tracks. Christian skulked back to our room, with one last black look in my direction. My father sauntered off.

That was the only time I spoke to anyone about the clock.

My mother was convinced that my brother and I needed different kinds of schooling. At our school, Christian complained about his boredom. There was little for me to complain about apart from having too much homework. No suitable option existed nearby (at least according to my mother) so it was arranged that he should start the new academic year at a well-known but distant boarding school. My father felt, as he did about so many things that happened in our family, that he'd been left out of the decision-making process, and he never disguised the fact that he was against this course of action. As the end of the holidays approached, my parents argued bitterly and often.

I suppose it was just another step towards their inevitable separation.

Early one cool and rainy morning, before it was fully light, my father set out for the train station with Christian. That was the last time I saw my brother.

We'd had an argument, and I regret that now. I didn't want him to go. Perhaps before that day, I had been in denial; it was true that I hadn't been able to think things through. As they left, I turned my back to the screen door in order not to see the car depart, although I couldn't help but hear it. I hadn't been able to face the inevitable awkward silences and tearful goodbyes, so I faced a few hours on my own.

What had the row been about? I had not even the vaguest recollection, and I tried not to guess. I doubt that my father or Christian would have known either. I spent much of my childhood feeling like I belonged to a different species from the rest of my family.

I don't know how long I stood with my back to the door, staring down the hall into the silent house. I wished my mother was home, but she had left even earlier that morning for yet another business meeting. It struck me then that it was the very first time I'd been alone in the house. I walked in slow motion down the hall and past the open door of what would be, from now on, my bedroom alone. Cold grey light fell across the unmade bed my brother had left so recently, exposing the wrinkled sheet which still bore the faint smudge of blood from his fingers.

The house was no longer silent. I had never before heard the clock ticking in the day, only during those bizarre night-time rituals. Christian was not here, and I was sure we still had no key.

The floorboards creaked and gave away my entry to the dining room. The morning was now darker, the clouds lower and the rain heavier, so I could barely see the imposing shape of the clock in the dimness between the curtained windows. I couldn't make out the hands on its face until I had made my way round the dining table. I felt uneasy. I was about to turn away when I noticed that the timepiece now stood on the floor, and that it had somehow grown to be taller than I was. Its door, now big enough for me to duck and step through, stood ajar. I felt compelled to open it wide. I stared at the industrious cogs, springs and wheels. I couldn't look away. Before long, my shoulders slackened and my eyes lost focus. In the absolute darkness around the clock's movement, shapes swirled and shifted. A familiar colour crept from the shadows. I recognised at once the cornflower yellow of the wallpaper in my nursery: one of my earliest and most intimate memories, from the family home we'd left behind several years before.

In front of me stood a cot, with a tiny shape tucked up tightly and wriggling deep inside. Warm sunshine, mixed with the heady smell of the lilac tree which dominated our garden, poured through the open window above my tiny bed at the other end of the room. I sensed the nursery door standing open behind me. The low murmur of voices from the landing beyond hung on the scented air.

I looked down at the knife I held in my infant hand.

"Let me tell you something, Rosie. You can't come back and expect to change what you did, just like that. The time has arrived for you to confront what happened. You need to face up to reality, and you need to do it now. If you leave it any longer, the passing of time will make things so much worse. For all of us."

It was my mother's voice, but young and clear.

"I don't suppose you've ever seen the very substance of time, have you Rosie? Have you witnessed a single second being born, living and then dying? Only once you've seen that very second clutching at life, and then screaming towards its own oblivion, will you understand that the essence of time can't be changed. It's not what we do that makes us suffer; the real tragedy exists within the fabric of time itself."

My mother's words rushed over me, yet I understood the warning they carried. Despite a growing sense of futility, I had convinced my childish mind that things could work out differently this time.

The scene shifted, and once again I was looking into the carcass of the clock. Something glinted from deep within, and I realised with an overwhelming sense of loss that it was Christian's watch, lying on its side against the back of the cabinet. I had to retrieve it, even if it meant leaning right inside. I was forced to thread my right arm between the pulleys, levers and wheels. My fingertips brushed the worn leather strap of the watch, but all I managed to do was to push it further away. Even at full stretch I could not quite grasp it. I made one last effort just as the whirring sound began, the preamble for the clock to strike the hour. I knew I should get out at once: however, the process had put a different set of cogs into motion, and I became trapped. It was possible for me to move further inside, but not to withdraw. I was wedged fast, and with every tick I was being dragged further inside. I squeezed my eyes shut in despair.

The clock stopped.

"Can you stop the pain?"

My eyes opened and I was in the nursery. My hand shook from the weight of the knife as I stumbled towards the cot, where small noises came from beneath the baby blue knitted covers. On the window above my bed, a shadow shifted, scraped and tapped. I could feel the light being sucked from the room and poured into my head.

"Do you think you can stop the time?" My mother's voice was loud, yet I still heard the conversation from the landing through the open nursery door. The harsh voices put my teeth on edge, yet they goaded me on. My face contorted with the effort as I tried to resist. I drew the blade slowly and almost tenderly across the doughy skin, and it brought me a wretched kind of relief.

A red rose bloomed on the pastel sheet. The scream separated me from my thoughts, and when they returned, they had been shattered into seconds when they should have been minutes. I was left only with the knowledge that I would be travelling along those familiar roads once more. It was foolish of me to think that I had the strength to cover any new ground.

It seemed to me that without Christian, there was little to keep my parents together, and it was not long before they divorced. My mother moved out. She said it was to be closer to her work, and I'm sure that was part of it. So, in such a short space of time, I lost two of the most important people in my young life. Over the months and years that followed, my father would occasionally give me rather vague news of Christian's progress at boarding school, and of how his greatest wish was to follow his mother into the world of finance. My own calling was more towards the artistic side of things. I was lucky enough to get an apprenticeship in sign writing, which led to both employment and independence. I had almost managed to put the clock right out of my mind. Until my father died.

I was living alone, renting a small flat on the very outskirts of Sydney, and I'm ashamed to say that I'd had no contact with my father for a number of years. I was preoccupied with building a life for myself, and I could see no reason to dwell upon the past. There were things I was running from, and tucked away at the back of my mind was the feeling that I'd had a lucky escape.

However, circumstances drew me back. I'd heard that Christian was living a life completely beyond my understanding, having followed mother upon her lucrative posting overseas. Once again it was left to me to perform the chores that my brother had always been shielded from.

So it was that I found myself trudging up the steep hill from the bus stop. I resented every step, and I was weary from the arduous journey on such a hot and humid day. The area had changed so much. Many of the houses down the street had gone, replaced by apartment buildings, already looking the worse for wear. Graffiti defaced concrete walls. Balconies overflowed with washing pegged to makeshift clotheslines.

I crossed the road and the bungalow came into view. It crouched into the side of the hill as it always had, and my first impression was that nothing had changed. The front door stood open, a mocking welcome after such a long absence. It was still the familiar Federation red, although as I approached, I could see its paint was both faded and peeling. The front lawn, which had looked so neatly trimmed from a distance, proved to consist entirely of sickly weeds. They smelt sour, and they had infiltrated the pathway, which was barely visible. The weeds had jammed open the rusty gate. My father had let the place go over the years.

Double-parked on the street out front stood an old black van, with its rear doors propped open.

I made my way up the ruined pathway to what was once my home. There was no longer a screen door to negotiate; only its rusty hinges remained, so I was able to step over the threshold and into the hall. At first, all looked much as I remembered. Even the old bureau stood against the wall just the way it always had. To my left, the door to what had once been my parents' bedroom stood open, and I had to brace myself to look inside. There was no bed, but there was no scene of devastation either. The wallpaper hung loose on the walls, and the floorboards were even noisier than I recalled, but that was only to be expected. I withdrew, relieved. I made my way into the only other bedroom, the one I had shared with Christian all those years before. That was also bare. My footsteps echoed.

Then I heard the clumsy movement from the dining room. I almost collided with the first of the four boys as they staggered through into the hallway. With their slack jaws and stares, they strained and sweated under the weight of the clock they carried between them. They had grown into stocky men, but they were less tall, far less tall, than the clock.

Eager not to impede their unsteady progress, I backed away, but not before I had a good look into the dining room behind them. The mess did not surprise me too much; oily rags and tools strewn around, cogs, springs and wheels littering the floor. However, that could not explain the smell, which may have been seeping through the huge cracks in the walls. I wondered also at the breeze blocks cemented into place right up to the ceiling in front of the windows, blocking out most of the light; it looked like the arrangement was meant to form some kind of shield. To keep something out, I wondered, or to keep something in? I shuddered. At that moment, I could not imagine ever entering that room again.

I continued backing my way out of the front door and down the path. It was only when I turned around at the gate that I noticed the small group of silent people behind the black van. I recognised old friends and neighbours who, impossibly, looked as they did in my childhood memories. Their heads were bowed (they were all dressed in their Sunday best) and none of them acknowledged me. I counted twelve of them. Meanwhile the four men slid their burden into the back of the van, then stood to either side. Several of the group threw flowers inside the van. Then, just as I knew would happen, Velasco appeared. His eyes met mine for the briefest of moments, then he tipped his shiny top hat in my direction and slammed the doors shut.

The van stalled several times as it pulled away up the hill at walking pace. I followed on with the cortege. The lazy heat of the sun slowed my thoughts, and I felt oddly at ease—at least, until we arrived in the shadow of the church. As they arranged themselves around me in a perfect circle, I saw for the first time the expression in their eyes. Only then did I understand there could be no escape from my past; and I realised the dreadful significance of there being *twelve* other mourners.

Paper Child

Sana Aslam

MR EVERSLEY LIKED to cut faces in his spare time. He liked odd ones best. Ones with podgy cheeks, beaked noses or Dickensian beards that grew square-shaped. He would hold up a small black card and a pair of fine scissors and glance at the guests in the drawing room. Then he would cut. Meanwhile, the sitters would tug at their collars and try to stay still.

'Done,' Mr Eversley would announce, thirty seconds later. He would peel away the sliced image, and his guests would gawp at the exact shadow of themselves caught betwixt his fingers. They would murmur praises and touch the perfect outline of their own nose, the curve of their hairline or their jutting chin on black card. Their eyes lit up in childish delight at recognising their own face.

Mr Eversley's daughter, Effie, understood this emotion well and loved to fold her arms over the top of her father's chair and watch him work. She was her papa's biggest fan. She had been since she was eight years old and had one day wondered out loud where children came from. Her mother spluttered and stopped, as though she'd swallowed a fish-bone. Mr Eversley paused. He wandered away to his study with a cloudy look in his eyes.

He reappeared in the drawing room before bedtime, cradling a paper tulip the size of his hands and ordered the scullery maid to fetch a bowl of water. He asked Effie to settle down beside him.

'Once,' said Mr Eversley, 'there was a man who greatly desired a child, but did not know where to find one.' Mrs Eversley snorted here, but her husband paid her no mind. 'He searched all over town, but to no avail. Until one day, he was given a tulip and told to plant it.' Effie tipped her head to one side. 'But this was no ordinary tulip,' said Mr Eversley.

He dropped the paper flower into the water bowl. It ducked and slid along the liquid, before settling in the centre.

'Watch,' said Mr Eversley. The corners of his eyes crinkled.

Effie loomed over the bowl.

The water tickled the flower. It yawned slowly and unfurled its petals to present a small roll of paper curled up in the middle. As the petals opened, the paper curl stretched out tiny arms and legs and became the shape of a girl.

'It's me!' Effie gasped. And it was. The silhouette had her sloping nose, her little pointed chin, and her curls tied up with a ribbon.

'Yes,' her father said. 'You wished to know how you came to us. You did so in a flower!'

'Isn't that one of Mr Anderson's stories?' Mrs Eversley accused.

'It's an adaptation,' said Mr Eversley.

'And where did you find me, Papa?' cried Effie, still looking at the girl in the tulip.

'I fought a witch to get you!'

Effie giggled.

Mrs Eversley scoffed.

'And I suppose I did nothing?'

More paper puppet shows were to come after the first, each one more intricate than the last. There was Peter Pan, who wore a tunic of tiny paper skeleton leaves, made jagged with the edge of a blade. He was attached to a string so that he could swoop over Effie's tulip boat and ask her if she were a fairy that had lost her wings, since she was so small.

'Come with me, and we shall sail your tulip-boat across the mermaid lagoon. Then I shall teach you how to fly,' said Mr Eversley, in a thin, boy's voice. He sat beside Effie on the drawing room floor, legs sprawled, hair dishevelled. Effie did not think he made a very convincing Peter, but she did not mind.

She cried when her paper tulip wilted. The petals drifted apart and her doll sank to the bottom of the bowl. It tore when she lifted it and crumbled between her fingers.

The next day her father conjured a new doll for her to play with and she was soon smiling again. She tugged him towards the drawing room, clamouring for his stories.

'I don't know why we even have a nursery,' said Mrs Eversley.

The silhouettes all ended up in Mr Eversley's study eventually. As Effie grew older, she was no longer permitted to play with the dolls. Marie's love for the Nutcracker Prince was only charming on stage, her mother said. However, Mr Eversley allowed his daughter to look at the dolls in his study. They dangled from strings attached to the ceiling in a shower of fairy tale scenery. Effie liked to sneak in at dusk and watch them glow blue in the moonlight. They swayed when she touched them and cast a painting of living shadows on the floor.

Her father's favourite, Peter, stayed by the window, under a cluster of stars. There was also a zoetrope of Effies. The wheel of paper girls held hands and whirled slowly in a ring. They began as a Thumbelina-sized

Effie and gradually got taller. Then stopped at sixteen and spun abruptly back into a child.

It was mid-December and the beginning of the social season when Mrs Eversley started shadowing her husband and daughter about the house.

Effie had grown up to be prettier than her paper child. She had slender hands, was skilled at the piano and had adopted her papa's love of making things. Mrs Eversley had to keep snatching the scissors away from her.

'Those paper cuttings are not suitable for a young woman,' she would say. 'And you must stop bringing them up every time a guest talks to you. Young men do not care for your flights of fancy.'

'They're Papa's creations. Not mine.'

'And that, too! You are no longer a child. Stop clinging to your father. Leave him alone when he is in his study. And address him as "Sir".'

'It's alright, dear. I don't mind Effie visiting the study. The puppets were mostly for her, anyway.'

'That isn't the point,' Mrs Eversley said. 'Effie is nineteen now. Yet you do not treat her like a debutante. She must attend more balls. I know you do not like them—'

'They're—'

'—loud, bothersome. I know. You prefer the company of intimate friends, but at least allow *me* to introduce her. The Wakefields have invited us to attend next Thursday.'

'But Papa was going to take me to the opera next Thursday!'

'Your father takes you to the opera every week,' said Mrs Eversley, sniffing. 'And even then you only stick to his side and refuse any other introductions. All you do is go to the theatre, then come back to the house and go about reading or cutting paper. No, you need to meet some people of your own class. You're coming with me.'

Effie pursed her lips and looked at her father. Mr Eversley only shook his head.

Thursday night, the scullery maids jumped when they heard what sounded like a beast from Baskerville enter the Eversley household.

'Effie!' Mrs Eversley boomed.

The two maids peeked out from behind the door to see Effie scurry along the halls. Her face was lowered. She clutched at her skirts and ran up the stairs. The women jumped again and scattered like mice when Mrs Eversley followed, continuing to shout for her daughter.

Upstairs, Effie twisted the ends of her silk gloves and stared at her bed.

She glanced up when she heard footsteps. Her mother stormed in like the Queen of Hearts, her petticoats hitched and face like a burning rose. Effie's heart plummeted into her stomach.

Her mother's breathing was ragged. She stood in silence for a moment, her stare cutting. 'Well,' she huffed, 'for a girl who fainted in the middle of a waltz twenty minutes ago you seem to have recovered *very* quickly.'

'I... I felt sick. I thought I should hurry.'

'Yes, because this is the only place you feel comfortable, isn't it? For goodness sake, Effie. If you were nervous you could have excused yourself to go to the powder room. Why make our host bring you back all the way here?'

Mrs Eversley pressed her hands to her face.

'This is disgraceful. The first ball of the season and we were there for only an hour. You did not even finish your dance with the young Master Wakefield. Y ou may as well have gone to your...' Mrs Eversley trailed off. Something appeared to flicker in her eyes. She finished, '... your opera.'

It was not yet eight. The opera house opened at nine.

'You...'

Effie had wrung her gloves until they were stretched and crumpled. She refused to look at her mother. She dropped her gloves and fumbled with something else. Mrs Eversley's voice cracked.

'I never ask anything of you, Effie. Goodness knows your father spoils you, allowing you to go about the house as you please. And you'll do whatever he says with a smile on your face, but God forbid I ask *one* thing of you!'

Tears pricked Mrs Eversley's eyes.

'I went out of my way to help you find a husband. To help you meet people. For once, I thought that we were bonding. You wicked, spoiled child. You did not wish to go to the ball with me. You only pretended to be sick so that they would send you home to your beloved Papa!'

Effie stopped her fidgeting and stood frozen in the centre of the room.

'I can no longer stand living in this house with you. You *are* sick, child. You and your father. It is a sickness of the heart. You dislike the company of others. You are selfish, care only for your fairy tales and your paper.' She was crying now. 'W—well, I cannot live like that. You may be able to live in a solitary house of paper, but I am made of flesh and blood and must be around other people.'

At last Mrs Eversley noticed something.

'What... what is that in your hands?'

There was an intake of breath. Effie said not a word. Slowly walking over to her daughter, Mrs Eversley tugged at the cut-out in Effie's hands and balled some of it in her fist. She lifted up the detailed silhouette of a horse and carriage. Effie's lips were pressed together. Her mother was mute.

Mrs Eversley turned on her heel and headed for the hall.

'Mama?' Effie said. 'What are you doing?'

'You and your father have never included me in your games. God knows I've tried to be a loving wife and mother. I don't understand it. It's lunacy. You are no longer a child and your father must stop believing he is Peter Pan.' Effie followed her mother down to her father's study.

'Mama, where are you going?'

'No more. No more games.'

The study's door burst open and the silhouettes whirled. Mrs Eversley grabbed a pair of scissors. Effie paled. All she could do was shake her head.

Only when the first, terrible *rip* sound tore through the study did she cry out.

Effie's father would not look at her afterwards. Effie sank to her knees and took her papa's hands in hers, but he jittered at her touch and folded them away, out of her reach.

From the other side of the door she could hear her mother ranting at the doctors.

'She's mad! She ran about with scissors and tore down all of my husband's work. See, she has hurt him so deeply that he cannot even speak. He just sits there!'

Tears streaked Effie's cheeks.

'You're cruel,' Mr Eversley murmured. 'I allowed you into my world and you ruined it. I can't bear to look at you.'

'Papa, no! You mustn't believe her, I—'

‘Go away, Effie,’ he said softly.

The doctors walked in.

‘Papa, please!’

Mr Eversley trembled mutely, clutching his head. A doctor took Effie’s wrist and led her down the hall.

She was stark white and silent when she stepped outside. Clouds gathered in the sky above. The doctor tugged her down the stone steps.

The edge of her dress darkened when it touched the wet pavement. It curled and bunched in on itself. The rain drops assailed her. The doctor that had her wrist started. Effie’s hand turned limp and thin and clung to him. He shuddered and tried to shake it off, but the hand remained pliant and stuck like a moth wing. When the doctor finally peeled the hand away it drifted down and hung at Effie’s side. Her skin became transparent and soft. He watched Effie’s body fold over at the waist and begin to crumple. She flopped silently onto the ground and became a pale wet sheet. The doctors ran inside for help, but when they came back outside all that remained were a few white flakes on the cobbled stone.

Hooky Pook

George Cromack

YOU COULD DO it then, but it wouldn't get away with it like that now.

Si stood with his catapult in his hand and took aim; it was like his Aunt had told us when the big 'toad king' kid snatched the girl's copy of *Look In* outside the shop on the way: 'he only wanted that because he could see she wanted it.' So that was his plan, not fool proof but we were thinking on our feet.

A pit stop at the post office, Aunt Emma marched inside. Si and I remained in the back of the Metro. The seats folded flat, cramped in amid allegedly antique 'stuff', we watched the 'village kids', as we called them. This was when the toad kid, as christened by Si owing to his smug wide mouthed appearance, made the magazine snatch. As a frizzy-haired girl and her flat-shoed friend made feeble protest, other village kids were drawn to the drama creating a procession trailing up a nearby grass mound whereby like a king the toad kid stood at the crown before ceremonially sitting on top of the magazine.

The driver's door opened. Aunt Emma had returned; she imparted her wisdom on the events witnessed and passed us a can of cola each. A couple of cranks on the ignition and we were on our way again. Si swigged on the cheap cola and belched; his Aunt eventually scolding him, using tales of his toddler days, for trying to eject the can's ring pull from the window. She told him to keep it on his finger until we went past a proper bin. Si obeyed but rolled his eyes at her anecdotal warnings. He didn't mind. He knew I'd never recall them at school. I'd spent a few summer days like this with Si and his Aunt—what happened on a jumble sale trip, stayed on a jumble sale trip.

We helped Aunt Emma set her stall up at the church hall, a long dark damp smelling room full of booming echoes. Once or twice when putting empty boxes under the table I was sure I could hear rats or something shuffling in the warped wooden wall panelling.

Si and I glanced around the other stalls, once we'd found an old Beano annual but no such luck today just dog-eared fishing magazines and old curtains. However, as we were browsing, cold stone eyes were also browsing us. Aunt Emma, had told us to keep a keen eye out as items were renowned for going missing at the sale.

Eventually, our stomachs rumbled and patience wore; an old egg cup hit the deck and smashed. Si was blamed although he swore he was nowhere near it. An elderly gent browsing some stamps was startled—we were entrusted with the car keys and sent away for an early lunch.

Egg sandwiches were discarded in favour of more cheap cola and crisps and mischief. Si rummaged under a blanket in the back of the Metro and produced his military catapult or so he always said it was. Used to belong to his dad apparently—dual coils of shiny steel tube precision curved into shape and a really thick strap of yellowish rubber cord to do the propelling.

We passed some time around the back of the church hall pinging pebbles at our empty cola cans. It was this sort of streak Si possessed which so often meant he missed break time at school but today was about jumble sale rules.

Our aim improving, inevitably we became too bold. Si tried for a trick shot with the intention to drop pebble into can. This failed and sent the can skimming at speed toward a previously unseen rat-tailed gardener.

The eventual deal was if we helped him to rake up his grass cuttings he wouldn't tell on us, to whom I still don't really know.

'You lads can't be scarin' easy, playing around *this* churchyard—suppose you know?'

We looked at one and other. 'No?'

The gardener perched on the old push mower and patted his overalls for his tobacco tin. Crafting a roll up he told us that back in the Second World War a wounded airman, flying over the village, jumped from a plane; his parachute becoming tangled on the church spire.

Left dangling until morning, he sadly died, the blood seeping from his wounds along the slates and into the church's guttering.

At this macabre detail, Si and I drew in closer.

A pause. 'You want me to go on?'

We were wide—wild—eyed.

He struck a match on the buckle of his motorcycle boot, sparked up, took a long drag and continued.

Turned out some said the gargoyle or grotesque on the church roof was bad news from the start, it being sculpted from an ancient *bullaun* stone that should never have been moved. Either way, it disappeared from the church roof after likely being splashed with the blood of the airman. Things around and about began to go missing, people started blaming it on that useless *hunky punk* or 'hooky pook' as it became known.

With a glance to his watch, the gardener began to pack his things away.

'Looks like rain.'

Casting down the fag butt; he left by telling us that it lived in the old potting shed from where it scrabbled around stealing bright things.

We weren't sure if it was right to want to believe him but, Si still had that streak of mind so we forced our way into the shed anyway.

In little time, amid thick layers of foggy grey dust, items loosely describable as trinkets were unearthed from behind some old draws. We leaned in closer: coins, shirt buttons, discoloured jewellery and even an old door knob. Curious, Si grabbed an old stamp. I was sure it was the very one the startled man was looking at earlier. Si licked his finger and stuck the stamp on the end.

It hardly seemed the most precious horde. We laughed, was this what they paid the gardener; inhaling vast quantities the musty air—I eventually let a powerful trio of sneezes ring out.

Si grabbed my arm.

'What was that?'

Still. We listened.

A stumpy hulk of stone came shuffling out from the shadows, the Hooky Pook itself; weather beaten grey skin with a shaggy mane of moss along its spine.

We were both struck by a sudden aching bolt of fear—was this really happening?

Somewhere in these frozen moments now lost to me we must've realised that, yes, it really was.

Next thing I recall we were halfway around the other side of the building making a manic get away, scrabbling around on the loose gravel as fast as our grubby Hi-Tec silver shadows could grip. Still juggling with our senses we both sat legs flat to the ground, arms tight to our sides and our backs pressed hard to a broad gravestone. Feeling a sharp sting, I glanced at my knee, a rip in the denim and a slight grazing to the flesh. I must've fallen in the mad scramble—it hardly seemed to matter. The gardener's words '*you lads can't be scarin' easy*' echoed in my head.

Si and I looked at each other, a shared unspoken 'reasoning', if we hid there just long enough maybe it would never have happened. Maybe there were rules like the Hooky Pook couldn't go out in the daylight or—something. Slowly we twisted our bodies around and teased our gaze over the gravestone.

The Hooky Pook was still there, hulking amid the gravestones at surprisingly quick pace in a zig zag manner, its head bobbing up and down as it took occasionally cover, its mossy grey hide almost camouflaged against the older gravestones. Worse still, not only was it still there but these tactical movements meant it was also stalking us across the churchyard.

Our eyes flashed around for the nearest escape from this twilight reality. No luck, almost cornered by a thick hedge and a tall Victorian era wall—the sort which still had the old bits of glass from broken bottles cemented along its top.

Si leapt at it, no chance—as his foot slipped and he staggered back into compost and hedge cuttings. The wind picked up and dashed fresh grass cuttings into our faces, rubbing our eyes—the Hooky Pook was still pursuing like an old barnacle encrusted shark on the scent of blood.

Searching for a reason, I told Si it probably just wanted the stamp back.

This was a pity as he'd long since let it go in the panic and a puff of wind.

The skies darkened. It began to rain.

Gaining ground on us, we noticed its head bobbling closer behind a large gravestone. I looked down, the damp grass making the grey dust stick to my trainers.

Si still had a ring pull on his finger—we had an idea.

He began to charm the Hooky Pook with the shiny ring pull still on his finger. It lingered like a cobra. I pointed to the church roof behind. Teasing it closer, Si drew his catapult and took aim.

The ring pull vanished skyward; I swear I heard a tinkling as it ricochet along the guttering.

A beat and the Hooky Pook shinnied up the drain pipe, tail like a powering pendulum, splintering slate, it edged to where the ring pull lay and grasped it tight—forever tight as the rain passed over and the water rooted it back on the building.

They stopped doing ring pulls here in about 1988. Like I said, you could do it then, but you wouldn't get away with it like that now.

<500

Tim Jeffreys and Martin Greaves

THE NIGHT USED to bring me disconcerting dreams which I couldn't make sense of but which filled me with warm feelings of love and comfort. They were dreams of another life, which might once have existed or which might exist only inside my mind. When I woke, staring into the dark, the feelings evoked by these dreams would remain in me until they were shattered by a sound. It might have been a shriek or a scream, or the muffled sound of weeping, or of someone begging for mercy. Whatever it was, it would make me sit up with a start. The comfort brought to me by the dream would be replaced by fear and confusion, emotions I'm used to. During the day, a few of the dream's images would stay with me and I would carry them around in my confused brain like someone else's memories: A child's soft blonde head; a woman's laughing eyes; a reassuring hand on my arm. Harradine tells me these images spring from my illness. They are a part, he says, of my madness.

These days, I no longer dream. Unless of course, this waking, as it sometimes seems, is the dream. But no. Not a dream. A nightmare.

Now when I hear those screams and cries in the night, what I mainly feel is gratitude. I'm grateful it's not my turn for whatever punishment is being meted out to the night's unfortunate recipient; grateful they are not my cries echoing along the dank corridors. I know, though, that my time will come. It will be a beating or an ice water bath—or something worse. Or I'll spend a few days in shackles, or deprived of food. Harradine says we should think of these things not as punishments, but treatments. But if this they are, then these men have discovered the very essence of treatment as interminable agony. I'm safe, for the moment at least, from further *treatments*. No more appointments with the doctor for at least a few days, since my injuries from our previous encounter, when they tied me to a cold table and cut gashes into my shoulder blades, *looking for evidence*, have still to heal.

There are more women here than men. There are children too, even babies. Some of them appear quite sane to me; you can see the clarity of thought which shows itself as a deep incomprehension in their eyes. Yet, for whatever reason, present society has decided they are lunatics and has locked them up here to suffer whatever treatments Harradine imagines will cure them. There are, of course, some genuine madmen and women among us. Take this fellow Durados for example, always shouting about how he doesn't belong here, how he wasn't meant to be here. *I'm not mad*, he screams, *I just don't belong here*. He shared my cell for a while, but they removed him after he became too boisterous. He used to call me *Captain*.

God knows why. Maybe he calls everyone Captain. He was always scratching at the wall with a bit of flint. He would always etch the same thing, a symbol and a number: <500. Over and over again, filling the walls with it. I tried my best to ignore him but Durados would insist on my complete attention to his ravings. He would look at me in this imploring way and say: *Yes? Yes?* As if I was supposed to understand what his insane scrawls meant. Then he would stare at me wide-eyed with expectation, pulling back his blistered lips to bare his broken teeth. *Jericho knew!* He screamed that over and over as they dragged him bodily to his new cell. *Jericho knew...!*

Then there was a woman in one of the rooms across the corridor who used to sing to me. I never knew her name. Or maybe I knew it and then forgot it. She'd hear me crying in the night and she'd start to sing—rallying, hopeful songs—until the guards came and silenced her. She was beautiful; at least, you could see that she had once been beautiful, before the grime and the bite marks, the bruises and the scars left by the treatments. Sometimes the guards would force themselves on her during the night when Harradine's back was turned, or when he chose to look the other way. All I could do was listen. She used to fight them, but she never won the fight, but she never gave it up either. Some might see that as proof of her insanity. The guards took a special pleasure in waking her up by emptying a bucket of cold water over her head. They enjoyed seeing her reaction to the shocking deluge as it blasted her face. She would scream and curse and spit and flail her arms at them. Anyway, she's gone now. Some new disease Harradine calls plague swept through the asylum some years ago and drastically reduced our numbers, made a bit of space to breathe out you might say. Lord alone knows why I was spared. I still hear that woman singing sometimes, in the dead of night when the bitter cold creeps in and the walls weep. The asylum is full of ghosts. I believe they will haunt this place eternally.

And Harradine, *doctor* Harradine—ha!—he tells me all about his qualifications. He tells me he is a physician and a theologian too, and that he is celebrated far beyond these walls, and that I should think myself lucky to be in his care! He says, too, that outside the asylum this epidemic is rife, that the population is dying, that it is being *judged*. That's how he puts it: the Bible being always closest to his hand rather than any medical or philosophical text. Either the plague will get you, he says, or it will be the pox. This was during one of our many talks. He likes to have me seated in his room sometimes, not for treatments or examinations, or to be screamed at by the emaciated monkeys that he keeps in cages, but just to talk. He said that he became fascinated with me because one night I saw the moon outside his window and told him that I had walked on it. He just laughed and laughed. But after the laughter subsided his face became clouded, his eyes bulged like there was some kind of internal pressure seeking to escape through the fissures of his skull.

What did you see there? On the moon? he asked, eyes ablaze.

Nothing, I told him. *Just a great empty world.*

He scribbled something down and then spoke of his own fascination with the moon, of how he would even plan operations to coincide with its cycle and its position in relation to other astral bodies. He told me he was *required by law* to do that! When I laughed he became extremely agitated. His anger would have been frightening had I possessed even an ounce of strength, but as he raved at me it seemed as if I was looking at him across some vast distance of time and space, and at points he faded to nothing more than a pinprick of light barely piercing my dimming eyes. He began to walk around looking at the various astrological charts that papered his walls, speaking of damnations and demons and things beyond comprehension; evil, sickening things. *Devils.*

He described a flaming star and how it had been seen traversing the sky for several days some years before. Harradine then looked me in the eyes and asked if I had ridden upon the back of that star. Whilst at first I thought he was mocking me, I quickly realised he was quite serious in his enquiry. Some minutes passed before I answered him, during which I brought my hand up to my temporal lobe and traced my fingertips across the rough scarring there. Doubtless the wound was caused by one of Harradine's treatments, though when it was inflicted, I cannot recall. Harradine waved an impatient hand in front of me, and I looked back at him and then I spoke in as steady a tone as I could muster.

No, I told him, *I had not ridden upon the back of that star.*

The doctor seemed keen to return to the subject of astrology and of the moon. I was growing tired, weary of the sensation that all of this was, to the physician, the ravings of a madman, stories told for his entertainment as much as his own personal investigative knowledge. *You can't imagine how it feels to be so far away from home,* I said—and then to my surprise I found myself weeping inconsolably. I could see that my spontaneous performance had aroused some innate curiosity in him, and my grief made those caged monkeys chatter, as if they found my distress pleasing. It must have seemed at that point more than any other that I had truly lost my reason. It wasn't sympathy that the doctor displayed, as such, it was more a form of pity; pity for this poor deluded, lunatic wreck he saw before him. That's why he gave me these writing materials, so I could, as he put it, *document my insanity*. Instead I treat the paper like a diary and fill it with mundane thoughts, which helps pass the time but which makes the doctor furious.

I beg him sometimes to tell me why I'm here, why I was incarcerated in this hellhole all those years ago. He replies quite matter-of-factly that I am in the place God intended me to be, but that it is his—Harradine's—duty to interrogate me and to discover exactly *why* I am here. He says I fell from the sky trailing a tail of fire, along with my companions. We were witnessed falling into the sea. He says that I must have been *cast down*! Then he asks me about *the Moor*. How was it that he was found with me? How could even a forsaken wretch like me deem to abide his Godless presence, and why did all of my companions insist on calling me *Captain*? Then he mused as to the possibility of my downfall being caused by one such as *him*: the Moor, the heretic. I confess I have no idea what he is talking about, and as for this Moor, this heretic, according to Harradine, that poor fellow perished two weeks into our capture when he attacked his guards. 'He was slain like the dog he was' was how the doctor related it to me, 'and his body burned on a pyre'. After moments in which he acknowledged my true bewilderment at his questions, the doctor adopted a more gentle tone. He, Harradine, was just an instrument, he assured me, a simple man doing the work of the Lord.

All of these words crackle in my brain; there's a sound of a rushing wind blowing in my ears and if I concentrate too hard I feel dizzy and experience the sensation of falling. It's like trying to recall a dream, but knowing that the fragments are indecipherable, that even if you could grasp them and join them together like so many jigsaw pieces, they would still make little sense. The spaces between would be too wide to form a readable picture. The doctor, the physician, the theologian, asks me what it was like to burn, what it was like to feel the Holy Fire engulf me as I fell. These questions frighten me, not because of the visions they conjure in my mind, but because I just cannot understand why he is asking them of *me*. Perhaps it is some form of new psychology, some random program of tricksy questions that seek to discover my nature through the answers I give to surreal enquiries. Whatever their insidious reasons, I'm not playing the game and Harradine can sense that. My statement about walking on the moon and my subsequent treatment in response to that utterance has taught me to keep my own counsel.

Apparently I had become very big news all about these lands, and Harradine asked me if I realised the tumult that had followed in my wake. Luckily the epidemic, (cholera, was it?) had wiped out so many people that the memory of me had died with them, my legend had been snuffed out like the living light of so many of those poor wretched souls who perished from the disease. But there were still men—very powerful men—to whom my appearance had caused considerable consternation, and it was these men who had caused me to be incarcerated here. Sometimes in my more lucid moments I could swear these men visited me in my cell, peering through my bars like paying customers at a freak show, but I was often too fatigued or too ill to take notice. To them I must have seemed beyond reason, the lowest depths of Man, the tattered remnants of a human being. Doctor Harradine was their tool; he reported back to them, it was his job to try to understand my nature.

It's a few days since I last wrote anything. My treatments have started again. This morning when they brought me back to my room I could not stand. They re-opened the gashes in my back; they seem to think I am incapable of dying! My mouth is so swollen that I cannot eat. The days here are endless, grim and without hope. I wish the cholera had taken me long ago. I am not improving; none of us in here are improving. Sometimes, I see another human wretch, usually as I am being led to Harradine's rooms, and as I glance at these shadows of women and men I am not altogether sure that they aren't ghosts. Surely no human being could be brought as low as this and survive? But then I look upon myself and realise that I am still alive, even though my will left me long ago. I still breathe, but my life force has abandoned me, I—like them—am a mere shell.

We are indeed forsaken, none of us will ever walk outside of these walls again, I know it. I'm an old man now. I feel ancient, like I am hundreds of years old and perhaps I am. Could I be immortal? Surely Death should have claimed me by now? I do not feel like writing at the moment. I wish I had a window in my room, one like

Harradine's, so at least I might gaze upon the night sky. I would like nothing more than to see the stars through these fading eyes.

Mission Alfred: 12th August 2042 – DataLog 1632TR/005217

We thought it best just to drift, to save as much fuel as we could for the return journey. In about twenty-two hours we'll reach the platform; the very edge of what we calculated as the safe zone from which to view this phenomena. From there we'll float right past that object itself and that's when we'll reconfigure the K54computerBank, or *Jericho*, to its designer, who named it after his youngest son who'd died in some terrible accident. Our hopes to interpret the tear rest almost entirely within *Jericho*'s carbon-graphene interior, where a coiled thicket of molecular tendrils pulse inside their crystal sheaths, relaying fifty-six million partecs-per-second, back to the *hive* at Ground Control. The whole package: a snip at two and a half billion dollars. While we drift, I might as well fill in some of the background about why we're here.

No one knew what it was, what had caused it, or why it was there. From the ground you couldn't see it, which was a good thing as there was no mass panic, no hysterical riots or people looting hypermarkets or biostations. You could imagine the scenes which knowledge of this might effect, the conspiracy theorists going into overdrive, the cults, the factions and the End-of-the-Worlders spewing their crazed crypto-religious nonsense, maybe even mass suicides on a global scale. Who knows what kind of behaviour the truth might have spawned, maybe nothing, maybe the Apocalypse. It was thought best not to tell the children. For the time being.

It was only visible on spectrum readings and had originally been discovered, almost accidentally, by a corporate probe in Sector 15, which normally transmits algorithms regarding solar flares from the surface of the sun. Using digital programming and IRIS Explorer 3d enhancement we could actually build a picture onscreen and see this thing with our own eyes and it looked like a fabric tear in the sky. The top brass worried about the night time because only at night could you make this thing out from Earth with the naked eye, but you would have to be looking hard, and only then could you perhaps make out a faint sheen or a flickering glint, like the moonlight reflecting on a fragment of black glass. Yet it was instigating widespread panic amongst the pool of scientists and military squareheads that were running this investigative program. Some people, rational people, thought it meant the end of everything and it surprised me how quickly they began to fear this unknown phenomenon. The reason for their disquiet was that this event didn't meet any of the criteria set out by the laws of physics. By all accounts it was an impossibility, it simply *couldn't* exist under the laws that governed our universe – and yet there it was.

The team of experts studying it was a mixture of age groups, from a whole variety of specialist scientific fields and nationalities. Most had a reputation for serious thought and informed opinion and yet there seemed to be an air of giddiness that infused the air, especially during brainstorming pods. There just seemed to be something about this...*thing* (strangely, nobody could think to call it anything else) something that connected with the primal fears that we all pretend we have conquered - that jittery, pit-of-the-stomach anxiety that even hard, brave men get when they look at something vast and unknowable and beyond reasoning. We were Neanderthals staring at fire for the first time. The only thought that was even more terrifying than the one we already felt was that it might be intelligent.

Our satellites and probes threw up nothing, which we found collectively astounding! There was so much hi-tech junk out there that the upper atmosphere resembled a carnival parade, and yet the most expensive, the most complex space hardware known to man, registered nothing but electromagnetic waves. These were waves of such enormous energy that many cities experienced power blackouts, after which hastily-scribbled press releases were thrown out to the puzzled media about erratic solar activity in an attempt to calm the populace, who might be enraged at missing their favourite late-night entertainment. One colleague even suggested that what we think of as the Spiritual, the *Rapture*, as the Romantics used to describe it in their poetry, was thought by many to be simple electromagnetic energy, the sacred soul as mere radio waves, and this threw up the ludicrous suggestion that this thing, this vast tear in space might be a portal to something sublime, a theory that resulted in quips about Saint Peter standing at the Pearly Gates. But they were jokes that met with uneasy laughter. The official line inside the loop was that no expense could be spared to look in detail at this strangeness, that if the probes threw no morsels our way, then we simply had to go up there and take a look ourselves, that it had to be investigated close up, face to face, *mano et mano*. A team would be trained up and then they would pilot a class 3 shuttle to mosey on up there and take a peek. When they approached me to captain the mission, I didn't know whether to be flattered or horrified.

“We just want you to cruise past, see if anything’s happening up there.” It was to be a fact-finding mission, nothing risky, they said, in a manner approaching outrageous understatement. Of course, I knew why they had chosen me. After I’d captained the *Spartan 2* mission; the ‘miracle mission’ as it had become known in legend, they couldn’t feasibly ask anybody else. But that’s another story. The Brass wanted me and in all modesty, I had to agree, there was nobody better suited.

Jayne wasn't inside the loop, this was too big even for family, even for wives, and anyway I knew what she would say. She’d say I had to think of Livvie and Mike, they needed their daddy around. She'd look at me in exasperation, she’d say I’d been lucky to come back from the *Spartan* debacle alive, she’d beg me not to push my luck one more time and ask why I couldn’t just accept my comfortable desk job, accept being Earthbound, and let others do the exploring. I would have been happy to give her what she wanted, despite my sense of duty to my country, to the world even. I was balancing the arguments in my head when they added a caveat to their request.

“We’ve got Collins on board already.”

“Collins?”

Jeanette Collins was one of the smartest people I had ever met. She had reached Fleet Grade 7 by the age of 22, a feat completely unheard of before then, and I knew as soon as I began mentoring her for piloting the B400s that she would go very far indeed, everybody knew it. Not only was she smart, she was strikingly beautiful, stunning actually, and possessed a wonderfully dry wit. She was perfect, but her personality was so natural, so easy, that she disarmed everybody she met, including Jayne, who might otherwise have regarded her with a wary wife's eye. Jeanette could have had any man she wanted. Jayne had once questioned me about her, albeit subtly and in her own beautifully measured tone, when we had been en route to our holiday at Hyannis Port, that first summer I mentored this gifted young cadet. Jeanette and I had become close during those training sessions, and I liked to think we still were, even though we only meet up once in a while these days. I don’t mean close in any kind of romantic way; it’s more of a father/daughter dynamic, I like to think. One day during the EMR training she took me aside and told me how much she admired me and how my escapades on the miracle mission had inspired her to become a cadet in the first place. I was quite stunned, since I’d come to feel exactly the same way about her. She was extraordinary, it just exuded from every pore, this girl was just.... *destined.*

She captained a moon landing when she was only thirty years old and that put her on everyone's radar. I'd heard on the grapevine that her name was being mentioned for the *Kronos V* mission to Mars, so just the thought of having her at my side for this particular assignment made me feel much more relaxed about it, or as relaxed as I could be. I had decided to tell Jayne it was a practice mission for *Kronos*, that I was mentoring Jeanette on some new Mars research equipment for a month-long test in deep space, and I hoped that would help convince Jayne, as well as ease her mind about me being hurled once more into the void strapped to an atomic bomb. Another factor, one I kept to myself of course was that if Jeanette Collins was already signed-up, well then, I wanted to be there beside her if anything should go wrong.

"And you know who else we've got? You'll like this."

"Yeah? Who?"

"Dan Durados."

If Collins' appointment hadn't already swung me, then this surely did. Durados was the greatest computer tech on the entire planet. He could look inside a computer the way an ECG can read your brain and he would know what it was thinking, amidst all the flashes and whizz-bangs. He had the gift. He was onboard because he was only one of three men in the world who could program *Jericho*, the other two being the original designer and the third being Durados again, because he reckoned he had double the brain capacity of anyone else he knew, and he was probably right.

"Show me the dotted line," I said. "I'm ready to sign."

Besides Durados, there was a final addition to my crew. I knew this guy was the leading astrophysicist in the field, and even though I'd never met him in person before, I was aware he had a global identity, something almost akin to a brand, and that most everybody knew *of* him, specifically through his bestselling books *The Astral Cartographer* and *A Billion Distant Suns*. He was one of those scientists that even housewives have heard of. Cab drivers discussed him. His name popped up in questions on popular quiz shows. He wrote books about the secrets of the universe in language that ten year olds could grasp. He was often on those magazine lists of the ten most famous people you would invite to a dinner party. People *loved* this guy. His name was Mohammad Khan, but he insisted that we call him Mo.

Jayne couldn't look me in the eye the night we left Earth. We stood out on the vast asphalt concourse so the children could look at our spacecraft *Alfred*, as it sat on the launch pad a mile away. Soft lights blinked on the enormous silhouette of the support complex and the blue gas of cryogenic propellants floated up from the umbilicals. I've seen that sight many times before but it always causes me to catch my breath. "Its so beautiful", Jayne said, and then her voice cracked and she cried and that's something she'd never done before. Perhaps she knew there was something else, something I wasn't telling her, and it wasn't about Jeanette Collins. It was something about the mission. She's my wife and even though we think we can keep secrets, perhaps we can't, not really. Not to those closest to us. She sensed something about me, something about my demeanour, an infinitesimal change in the familiar atoms that formed me, that caused her instinctively to fear for my wellbeing. The children gave me a hug and plenty of kisses, and that helped to calm her, the normality of a simple goodbye. I could have been going to the store for a quart of milk. I was a hero to them, my children. Livvie said, "I love you daddy!" and as I told her I loved her too I caught a brief glimpse of a dull glint high up in the night sky.

Collins' parents were there to wave her off. I could see how proud they were of their little girl. And there was a man, a very handsome man. Of course there was. He took Jeanette in his arms and looked as if he would never let her go. I felt something like jealousy, though I would never have admitted it to anyone, including myself. I made a mental note to ask Collins about this new man in her life later on, but I also made an addendum to moderate my tone to one of nonchalant indifference in the asking. It would be listed under *small talk*.

The shuttle ignition sequence ended and a craft that, fully fuelled, weighed 6.5 million pounds (or 3,000 metric tons) and had a payload capacity of 260,000 pounds, was thrust slowly off the launch pad by huge engines with a combined total of twenty-two million horsepower, expelling 7,648,000 pounds-force that lifted us beyond the confines of our atmosphere and out into the gaping maw of blackest space. Once we had switched off the boosters and hit zero G, we lost no time at all in cranking up K54 to run preliminaries. Durados fussed around *Jericho*, like a dedicated father. He didn't so much program the computer as *commune* with it, it was something approaching paternal affection, and as I remembered the dead son of its creator, the sight of Dan whispering thoughtfully to this elegant machine was almost touching. But in those first few hours we got nothing. Even the advanced computing brain of gazillion-dollar *Jericho* was completely stumped.

I have to stop typing now. Mo has just entered to tell me we're getting close to what we have recently begun to call *the Rip*, so we have to reconfigure *Jericho* and start our readings. The next few days will be busy ones for all of us. May God be with us.

Mission Alfred: 14th August 2042 – DataLog 1632TR/005218

Thirty-six hours have passed since my last entry. Something extraordinary happened which I will attempt to describe. We were approaching the platform; Dan Durados was busy running analysis through *Jericho* and had processed every available scientific theory thrown up by the brainstorming pods. *Jericho* was transmitting quantum mathematic equations back to the *nest* which the team back on Earth was pouring through like the ultimate cabal of boffins working out the Universe's most complicated crossword clues. Durados was hitting the keypad so fast I couldn't accurately make out his fingertips as they appeared to be engulfed in fog as he ran bizarre combinations of the whole gamut of the Periodic Table's list of known elements through the computer's substantial t26cortex. Finally, *Jericho* had stepped up to the plate and was offering us some slightly confusing data, which nevertheless suggested changes in the positioning of the Rip itself. Jeanette Collins, Mo Khan and myself were making sure that the ship's course would take us straight past the Rip, but not anywhere too near. With the possibility of significant changes in the structure of the Rip being caused by the ship's approach, we just couldn't risk crossing the safety of the platform's boundary. Close up, the Rip looked more like a pristine triangular shard, with a dull metallic light emanating from within and the edges rippling like molten lead; the sight of it made me very uneasy, so I was making sure our co-ordinates were spot on. No mistakes.

All of a sudden and without any warning from any of the onboard computers, including the priceless *Jericho*, the entire cabin was flooded with the most intense light and a cold wave went down my back as I detected some new force affecting the shuttle's course, pulling it to the right, pulling it towards the Rip. I shielded my eyes from the x-ray beams, but the piercing glare penetrated right through to my retinas and I found myself staring through the gossamer curtain of my eyelids, beyond the flesh of my bicep to see the Humerus of my left arm bisecting my vision like a blue/grey crossbeam. The traction I felt on my entire body was more than an invisible magnetic force; it seemed *physical*, like a huge sea serpent had somehow wrapped itself around us, around the shuttle and around all of us individually inside the hulk of our spacecraft. Collins and I looked at each other with the same stunned face, both of us realising at the same moment what was happening, and that we were powerless to do anything about it whatsoever, because we just couldn't move. We were in a state of paralysis and were reduced to staring mutely at one another like so many krill floating silently inside a jar of seawater.

It's pulling us in. I thought, and I saw my children's' faces in front of me. I felt their arms wrapped around me, but it wasn't their arms, it was the serpent's coils and it was crushing my chest cavity, squeezing the air from my lungs. I looked at Dan and his eyes were almost on stalks, his face puce coloured. Khan had passed out and hung there limply, like a puppet whose operator had left him dangling by his strings. Collins stared at me. Her eyes were wide, but she was remarkably calm. I think she actually smiled at me. Then, the ship lurched, like it had wrenched itself free of its bonds and we were thrown to the floor in unison.

"Fire up the boosters!" I shouted. "Full force! NOW!"

All four of us were trained to remain calm, but it was the three of us who flew at the control panels, because Khan remained prone on the floor, a look of blessed oblivion wrought across his slack face. He was alive though. The rest of us dashed about the cockpit, pressing buttons and pushing levers almost by instinct, our training allowing us to perform actions almost before our brains had thought of them. But nothing we did seemed to work. We were moving closer and closer to the Rip. At some point I stopped and looked out of the cockpit window, and all I could see was a bright white light, it was like we were colliding with the centre of the sun and some recess of my imagination imagined the people of Earth bursting into some kind of spontaneous combustion as the intensity of this illumination baked the planet like delicate flower inside a blast furnace. I thought of Jayne and Livvie and Mike, but their faces bleaching out in the glare of the light like overexposed photographs as I flailed back towards the controls. Those moments seemed like a lifetime and in the midst of them I had some mad idea that I should have refused the mission, and in that brief moment I felt like a coward.

After staggering around the cockpit, shielding our faces from the intensity of the glare, the light suddenly dimmed, as startlingly as it first exploded into the cabin. It was like a spent flashbulb dying. When I removed my hands from my face, the shuttle's interior was once more lit solely by its own electrical illumination and that bright white light had completely disappeared. Durados stepped forward to look at *Jericho*'s glaucomic computer screen, just as it started going crazy. Figures and letters were filling the screen. They scrolled so rapidly it made me feel nauseous to look at them; they were an illuminated blur, a cascading strobe of funfair lights on a midnight rollercoaster ride. The printer came alive, spewing out complete gibberish and seeming to scream as it did so, though it was obviously the interior cartridges squealing back and forth across their scorched aluminum tracks. An odour of burning filed my nostrils. I turned to Collins who was looking intently out of the side window.

"I can't see the Rip," she said. "It's gone. But I can see the Earth. Thank God. We're exactly where we were when we started to get sucked in. For a minute I thought we might be on the other side of the Universe." She laughed, more to relieve the tension than anything else.

Dan Durados was jabbing at *Jericho*'s computer panel, trying to get it to stop its babbling. If before, Dan had seemed like a parental figure, now *Jericho* was like a spoiled child throwing the biggest ever tantrum and Dan was the frantic father trying to placate its volcanic fury. He said he needed to filter out all the nonsense and find some decipherable data, some indication as to what had just occurred. At one point he actually *shushed* the manic machine, and then he looked back at me and laughed too. For a second the K54's display went blank, and then a single message began scrolling up its garish screen:

<500.
<500.
<500.
<500.
<500.
<500.

"What the hell does that mean?" I shouted at Dan. He only looked at me and shook his head. Dan Durados didn't know what the computer was saying to him. For me, that was the single most terrifying moment of this entire mission.

We administered some medical treatment to Khan, who awoke sporting an epic headache and a sprained wrist, but thankfully nothing more serious. It took him another hour to come around properly and we then described the events with the Rip to him. He had no explanation to offer at the time, *not too much material for your new book here then*, I thought, but he looked anxious enough and though I didn't like what I was reading in his expression, I let it go – there was too much to do. I joined Collins at the side panel window. What she had said was true, we were still at the boundary of the platform, but the Rip was no longer where it had been, in fact it had vanished completely. But the Earth was there, clear enough. That beautiful blue and white orb floating in a sea of black. Home.

"Fire up the boosters," I said for the second time, "Contact Control."

"Where are we going, captain?" asked Collins.

"This fucking mission is aborted," I said. "We're going home. I want to see my wife and children. I want to tell them how much I love them."

Collins grinned at me and said, "Aye, aye."

Mission Alfred: 14th August 2042 – DataLog 1632TR/005219

I am writing this log in my quarters, I cannot raise any communication with Ground Control and all attempts to contact them are met with incessant static. I think its important to write as much as I can whilst it's still fresh in my mind, and anyway, I can't know if *Jericho* will ever manage to provide us with any meaningful data. Perhaps we should ask for our money back. Durados told me that the K54 is still repeatedly scrolling **<500**, whatever the hell that means. He says it's like a lunatic, babbling out the same fucking sequence over and over. He said if *Jericho* was actually human, he imagines it would be crouched in a corner, nodding its head and rocking. He said it seemed.... *traumatised.*

Alarms going off all over the place. Looks like Dan has computers back online.

End of log.

Shuttle ALFRED EMCR52 onboard:data.<2042/// TERMINAL66664485685688.99888.

RECONFIGURE TRAJECTORY-COORDINATES 36degrees north/north west-64 degrees south/south angle of decent override. SECT455

676478438Y7478T78 FUELGAUGETORQUE@45

MINUS 63 SUGFE787R3 G33374578458G4G45G4G47
ALL SYSTEMS FAIL
ALL SYSTEMS FAIL
ALL SYSTEMS FAIL
ALL SYSTEMS FAIL
ALL SYSTEMS FAIL
ALL SYSTEMS FAIL
7632R73RT857TY 59TY54945 T Y9458T Y45T 4OT4Y5TY 4764565467
INITIATING TRAJECTORY OVERRIDE
CRITICAL
CRITICAL
CRITICAL
CRITICAL
BOOSTERS AT TERMINAL VELOCITY
SHIELD FAILURE
LIFE SUPPORT @ 22% drexl153465467676578
OXYGEN LEVEL @ 33.05555% drexl3t65655876565
FAIL
FAIL
FAIL
FAIL
FAIL
PREDETERMINED FAIL LEVEL 6
LIFE SUPPORT @ 12% drexl546546754765898
EMERGENCY LIFE SUPPORT INITIATED
ESCAPE POD SEQUENCE 79% COMPLETE
DOCKING STATION 2 ACTIVATED
POD COORDINATES LOCKED
HATCH LOCKED
ESCAPE POD SEQUENCE 84% COMPLETE
RELEASE HAMMERHEAD LOCKING BOLTS
INITIATE VALVE SUPRESSION SYSTEM
ESCAPE POD LIFE SUPPORT READINGS @100%
ESCAPE POD SEQUENCE 100% COMPLETE
RELEASE ESCAPE POD
ESCAPE POD RELEASED……………………………………………

Great Uncle Eltwood

Matthew M. Bartlett

WHEN THE CALL comes, it's never at a convenient time. In this instance, it was at 4p.m. on a rainswept Saturday in late November. My great uncle, having lived to the improbable age of 102, had apparently finally worn down the staff at Brookside Willow Pavilions with his increasingly loud and incoherent and doleful jeremiads, and the Board of Directors had voted to unceremoniously "release" him. I argued on the phone, employing every cliché (where is he supposed to go, you can't do this, etc) and inventing some new ones.

But I understood from the start the effect on people my uncle could have, even when well. After all, as long as I'd known him, his ideologies and religious affiliations changed like the New England weather, and each change came with an oft-repeated speech. The man couldn't go a month without a new epiphany. And rather than gather the family 'round, he'd corner you at a reunion and regale you with the speech you'd heard him give Aunt Asenath at breakfast. Verbatim almost, but with each new iteration a change here and there...a comedian "improving" his act. He'd even execute a self-deprecating laugh or a knowing shake of the head...at the same spot each time.

The person on the other end of the phone was a dispassionate, obdurate bureaucrat with a resonant voice—an old time broadcaster's vibrato. No, the decision had been made and was final and I, as the sole heir to this particular misfortune, had no choice but to drive from New York up through to central Vermont to fetch my great uncle and his meagre belongings. Now. And he had no one left but me.

A few phone calls to work and family across the ocean, and I was off. I drove between the sodden trees and frowning awnings lining East 79th Street and wended my way through the drizzle-hazed, Creamsicle-coned streets, and onto the FDR. By the time I hit 95 North, the drizzle had stopped but all was still black and white. The radio—alternating between talk and music—kept me company and awake during the first part of the trip up through Connecticut, then I added a strong, large coffee somewhere south of Hartford. A duo, I thought, coffee and radio, working to keep my car on the road.

But then, a few miles before the border of Vermont, the radio bailed on me. A rental car without satellite or a CD player is what you get when you call at 4:30p.m. on a weeknight, and that's when I'd called. So now, as night really settled in, and the coffee began to wear off, I settled into a serious fret. I needed more coffee, but I couldn't remember the last time I'd seen an exit, or a street sign for that matter. But I resolved to keep going, and I did, pretty much until the point when I realized that going back to the last exit with Food signs would put me too far off schedule...and I wouldn't be able to do it anyway until another exit came along. So, if no coffee...I spun the radio dial back and forth melodramatically, finding only varying keys of buzzy static. I cranked the volume, hoping the static might form into music or words.

I didn't care what I would find—talk, sports, any kind of music. Just a voice, please, or a musical note. A zither's strum, an accordion's bleat, the plastic thump of an electronic drum...a goddamned SOUND. For five minutes straight I begged the radio aloud, just to hear my own voice...and then the dissonant chord of a church organ sounded so clearly and loudly that I briefly lost control of the car. Someone watching would have thought I'd had a stroke, I thought, but the idea of someone watching in the middle of nowhere, from the towering woods...well, that was something I didn't want to think about. I wrested the car back into the travel lane with one hand and spun back down the volume with the other.

"Through him...in him...with him...in the unity of the holyyyy spiiiiiriiiii..." warbled a male tenor, a very familiar doxology, though I hadn't been in a Catholic church since the age of thirteen. Then the priest's voice faltered, rasped, and disintegrated into a violent coughing fit...wet, hacking, productive coughs, by the sound of it. On and on it went, until the reel-to-reel at the station must have begun to fail. The cough slowed to a low, monotonous drone, then sped up slightly, faster, chirpily fast...then reversed...backward coughing for a time, then backward singing, with that lispy, hissing sound like the tongue of a serpent caressing the microphone with unspeakably foul intent. Then the loop stopped as though the reel had been violently dispatched, and after some thumping and clacking, organ music resumed, a climbing, sing-songy, carnival tune. Occasionally it reversed for a time and then righted itself, providing a disquieting soundtrack as I drove through the dark night, the walls of the woods rising higher and higher on either side of the unlit interstate. I had seen no highway signs. Even the painted stripes were gone. Blacktop, woods, moon.

The road does tend to hypnotize one, and it certainly did me. I fear I slept awake, dreaming and driving, for exactly how long I'm afraid to speculate. What woke me up, I thought, was drums...which is an odd accompaniment for pipe-organ music, to be sure.

But then I looked to my right and saw two reined and harnessed black horses galloping madly alongside, kicking up gravel. The hooves were bass drums, the gravel tapping my window was tom-toms and snares. The nearest horse's eye rolled toward me...it was red-veined and wide, and full of terror. I hit the accelerator. Their muscled torsos strained in the moonlight as they began to pass me, their heaving sides, their lashing tails...and then a black stagecoach, shaped like a squared-off heart—a curtained window; a low, windowed door; another curtained window. On the roof, strapped-in luggage, ancient and tattered. My car swelled with sounds: pipe-organ, rising, rising; the thundering hooves and ricocheting gravel, the creaking, clattering carriage; the hysterical whinnying. Then ahead, I saw a street sign, the first I'd seen in miles. It was a red, reflective diamond and it read, BUMP. My car, and then the carriage, hit what felt like a ramp. My car left the ground and slammed back down. I heard a tire go. Alongside, the carriage rose and descended. When it came down and hit the pavement, the door flew off, hitting the rear of my car and spinning into the darkness. Spokes cracked and flew from the tires, splintering as they hit the pavement. One speared a horse in the flank, and it shrieked horribly as blood spurted in a great arc. The trees blurred by, smudged thumbprints smeared over impenetrable thicket.

Then the whole carriage leaned like a house of cards, squealing, nails popping, faults gaping between the boards. I saw with mounting horror what had been revealed when the curtains were torn from the windows. In the front, in the driver's seat, was a goat with nubs for horns and giant, gravestone teeth. I'm going mad, I thought. The goat wore a tall hat. A monocle on a chain sat over one eye. As he struggled, his hooves pummelling the wheel, I saw beside him another goat, shrieking, one ear soaked in blood, massive teeth, wide eyes. Lipstick was smeared ineptly about its lips. It wore a woman's frock and pearls. Then the horses began to gallop faster, and I saw into the rear window. Man and woman, human, middle-aged, freshly dead, their hair and jaws bouncing in time to the careening carriage, their purple tongues swollen, protruding from their mouths. Their teeth were shattered, their eyes staring, unseeing. As I watched, the carriage disintegrated, goats and humans spilling into the road like dolls in the wreckage. The couple was naked from the waist down. Suitcases skittered across the road, opening, spilling clothing. The wounded horse pushed out its front legs straight, and they broke with horrible cracking sounds. The horse collapsed, and the other dragged his partner hitchingly into the darkness, their shrieks echoing through the trees.

I stopped my car and sat in silence. The radio was quiet, my heart beating madly, pushing at my ribs. I opened the door and stepped out onto the highway. It was suddenly so quiet and still...just the sound of one detached wheel rolling in decreasing circles at the shoulder of the road. And then I saw the faces...in and among the trees...children, mostly, some young adults. Their faces were white...a grim diaspora of the damned. The wind ruffled the leaves and their hair. They were whispering, all of them. It sounded like rain. I walked toward them, and they faded back into the woods as though the group had all slid quietly backward into the dark. I continued until I saw them again...and they faded again. And again. And again. I trod through the underbrush, my shoes squishing in the mud, until after about ten minutes I saw a dull yellow glow. I followed the glow into a small clearing. Ringing the opposite side, the faces hung in and among the trees, gape-mouthed.

Before me hovered three goats bathed in moon-glow, the middle one slightly higher than the others. They wore dulled red and white robes, and their expressions were beatific. Flies buzzed around them, lighting and then taking off, lighting again. The middle goat's forearm was pointed at the sky, her hand the delicate, small hand of a young woman. Her middle and forefinger pointed up, the ring finger and pinky pointed down, against her soft palm. Her feet dangled from the bottom of the robe, toes wiggling absently. Her goat's mouth quavered, and then the jaw moved up and down as though she were speaking. I leaned forward, but heard nothing except the filthy buzz of the horseflies. Her eyes, those queerly-shaped goat pupils, fixed upon mine and held them. Then she grinned, all huge teeth and blister-flecked tongue. H er eyes blinked heavily.

They rose, the three of them, up into the fog, and were gone. The grey faces faded back into the trees. Whatever this was, it was over, no word spoken. I returned to the car. It started, and I drove off, slowly, the radio off.

Before long, I saw lights lining the highway ahead, and soon an exit sign. I walked into a Sunoco's too-bright food mart. On the radio a woman over-emoted to generic R&B. I went into the restroom and regarded myself in the mirror. My hair stuck up in spikes, and the familial dark circles around my eyes were darker than normal. Otherwise, I was me. For whatever that was worth. I splashed my face with water, grabbed a limp sandwich smothered like a murder victim in plastic wrap, and got back on the highway.

An hour later I exited the highway in Central Vermont, the mountains looming high above me. I drove through a sleeping suburban complex of wide, white houses with broad porches, some surrounded by expansive and neat hedges, and turned into the driveway of Brookside Willow Pavilions. I got out of the car. My legs were shaky and I felt very tired and overwhelmed. It felt like a chore just to walk. I opened the double doors.

The lobby was empty. A desk with a phone and a computer was angled in the middle of the room; to the left of that on a podium sat a guest register with a few scribbled names and times. There was no receptionist in sight. Somewhere down a hall echoed upsetting percussive sounds I could not identify. I signed my name and that of my uncle—Eltweed—and started down the hall toward the crashing sounds. The door to Section C, where my uncle resided in one of fifteen cheerless bedrooms arrayed around a grand piano and constellation of chairs, had a light brown hand-print on it. I somehow immediately identified it as butterscotch pudding. I opened the door, and the crashing sounds stopped.

The lounge area, usually buzzing with residents reading the paper or nodding in front of half-done jigsaw puzzles or staring into space, was empty. I saw no aides or servers. Magazines lay fanned out on end tables. A dying flower sagged in an empty, dusty vase. Then I heard a titter from the dining area. I went around the piano and into the L-shaped room. My uncle sprawled in a large easy chair where the dining room table was supposed to be, clearly quite dead—a mannequin conceived in a madhouse. What was left of his grey hair formed a cloud around the back of his head. His jaw hung at his chest and his eyes showed only whites. He was clad in a fly-blown bathrobe and striped boxers whose front lay alarmingly open. Between his feet sat a transistor radio, spitting staticey gypsy jazz. Sitting on each of his wiry, bare legs was a dark-skinned aide. One was plump, in tight fitting grey sweats. The other, in an evening dress, was wasp-waisted and hard-faced. Both were Dominican, both grinning wickedly. The plump one looped her tongue over and around his large left ear, and then bit, hard. My uncle came to life, his eyes rolling back into place, and

The Ressurection Spell

Tim Jeffreys

ALWAYS ON A WEDNESDAY, and always by accident, Martha met with Mrs Collingwood. Sometimes they saw each other in the street, or at the bus stop. Once they had risen from their seats at the same moment to get off the bus, recognised each other, and laughed; both having been so wrapped up in thought that they had spent the entire journey sitting opposite each other without realising.

One Wednesday in May, they met as Martha was leaving the florist she always stopped at. Seeing the old woman making her way up the street, she smiled. Mrs Collingwood returned her smile, nodding at the small bouquet of flowers and the little teddy bear Martha cradled in her arms.

"Off to visit your Owen again?"

"I am," Martha said. "And you? Going to see Arthur?"

"Every Wednesday."

"And what've you brought for him today?"

Mrs Collinwood raised the carrier bag she held in one hand. "Small bottle of whiskey. He always liked a drop of whiskey, Arthur did. The good stuff."

Martha laughed. She waited for Mrs Collingwood to reach her, and then fell in step with her. Though the sun was shining, it felt chilly in the shade. Together, they crossed to the sunny side of the street, took a left turn and passed inside the cemetery gates.

Here, alder trees set beside the path blocked the sun's light. Martha rubbed at goosebumps on her arms. They walked the path between the graves until the old woman broke the silence, saying in a flat voice:

"There's so many of them."

"Yes, it's so sad," Martha said. She'd been thinking the same thing, looking from side to side at the rows of graves. "I'd like to bring them all back to life. Imagine if there was a way to do that. Wouldn't it be wonderful?"

"Like zombies you mean?" Mrs Collingwood said.

"No, I mean like they were. Just restore them back to the way they were."

"Could get awfully crowded. Anyway, here's my Arthur. I wouldn't mind having him back, out of all of them. Is that selfish?"

"Of course not."

Martha watched as the old woman left the main pathway and followed a smaller trail towards the spot where her husband's modest headstone stood. The old woman took the little bottle of whiskey from her bag, presented it to the grave as if for approval, then crouched and placed it against the headstone.

"There you are, Arthur. There's your whiskey."

Martha, still watching, felt a lump rise in her throat.

"You go on, dear," Mrs Collingwood said, not looking up. "Owen's waiting. I'll see you on the way out. Take your time. Do what you need to do."

"All right. See you shortly."

Martha turned and continued, head bowed, along the main path. In time she came to a small statue of an angel beneath which was the grave of Owen John Jones. She stared at the grave for a while, before placing the flowers and the teddy bear down upon it. She then went and sat on a nearby bench. She stared at the statue, feeling as if she too were made of stone. She used to cry, coming here, but now there were no more tears, just a feeling of numbness. She felt guilty about this. There ought to be a few tears, even after all this time. Could it be that she was forgetting him? She tried to picture his face in her mind, but it was indistinct. How could she forgetwhat he looked like? She told herself she would take down the box of photos from the top of the wardrobe when she got home that evening and look through them to remind herself. Then she decided, *no,* she was not going to do that. The last time she had done that she had cried for a week.

"You were my little boy," she said softly, to the statue, to the breeze, to no one. "And I miss you every moment of every single day. I wish that I could hold you in my arms, just one last time."

All around her there was silence.

Later, after following the path back towards the cemetery gates, she found Mrs Collingwood sitting on a bench. Nearing the old woman, Martha smelled liquor.

"Shared a drink with my Arthur," Mrs Collingwood said, seeing the look on Martha's face. "There's no harm in it."

"No, of course not."

"Helps dull the pain."

"I know."

Martha wanted desperately to escape the shade of the alders and step out into the spring sunshine, but the old woman walked slowly.

"How old was Owen when he died?" Mrs Collingwood asked.

"He was six. He ran out into the road and...a car...it..."

"It must have been a very difficult time for you."

"Yes. It was the most awful time of my life. My husband — Owen's father — blamed me. I think because I was there when it happened. I wasn't paying attention. Just for a moment I wasn't paying attention. But it wasn't...I mean...I couldn't...Anyway, he blamed me. He couldn't stand to look at me anymore, so he left. That was hard. And I had to grieve. Years and years of grieving." She turned her head to Mrs Collingwood, giving a wan smile. "See these grey hairs?"

"It takes a long time to get over a loss like that. My Arthur was eighty-six when he upped and left me. He'd lived a good long life. It still hurt. Losing him was like losing half of myself. I was so used to having him around. Strange, the ways you miss them. But to lose a child must be the hardest thing in the world. Here," Mrs Collingwood ducked a hand into her handbag and produced the little bottle of whiskey she'd brought for her husband. It was almost empty. "Have a drink."

Despite herself, Martha took the bottle and drank from it. The liquor blazed in her throat and chest.

"Feel better now?" Mrs Collingwood said. "Just a little?"

"Maybe a little," Martha admitted. She was silent for a time, before saying, as she looked around, "Imagine if there was a way to bring them all back. A magic spell or something."

Mrs Collingwood chuckled. "Well, if you ever find one, you be sure to bring my Arthur back first, okay? You promise me."

"Oh, I promise," Martha said, with such sincerity that Mrs. Collingwood laughed again.

"I was pulling your leg, dear. There's no way to bring them back. What's gone is gone. They're in a better place now."

"You think so?"

"I hope so."

They passed through the cemetery gates. Martha was grateful for the warm sun on her skin. As Mrs Collingwood made for the bus stop, Martha turned in another direction.

"Not getting the bus, dear?"

"No. I think I'll walk. It's good for me."

"Oh. All right, dear. See you next Wednesday?"

"Yes, see you then."

With a smile for each other, the two women parted.

Martha had hoped the long walk would clear her mind, but when she arrived home she felt weary in her body, and thoughts were still turning in her mind: if only she had done this, if only she had never done that. It was no use. Outside it had clouded over and her house was full of dull light and silence. Sighing, she pulled a chair up at her kitchen table, remembering what Mrs Collingwood had said to her in the cemetery: *What's gone is gone.* It was true. When would she ever accept it? Accept it fully?

Lifting her head, she gave a little exclamation and smiled, despite herself, seeing that the potted geranium she had nursed all winter (though the leaves had ultimately shrivelled and turned brown), was now back to rude health and starting to flower. When had that happened? She lived some days in a kind of daze, going through the motions but not noticing anything about her.

Well, she thought, *if I can bring that back to life, why can't I–* She stopped the thought in its tracks. It was no use thinking like that. If she went on thinking like that she would never feel better. *Just accept it,* she told herself. *Accept it. Move on.*

Would it hurt, though, to go to the library tomorrow and look for some books on magic that might...?

No. That's ridiculous. What's gone is gone, like Mrs Collingwood said.

Sighing again, she forced herself to her feet and got busy preparing supper. After a few moments she stopped.

The pictures. I need to look at the pictures. I'm forgetting his face. I can't forget his face. I shouldn't.

No, don't do it. Not now.

I need to look.

Setting the ingredients for the pot roast down, she walked out into the hall and into her bedroom. She pulled a stool up beside her wardrobe, climbed on it, reached up, and felt towards the back of the wardrobe. After a few moments searching, she located a shoe box which she took down and carried to the bed.

Sitting and opening the box, she knew at once she'd made a mistake. She couldn't stop herself though. Some awful compulsion made her take out the photographs and look at them, one by one. After only a few minutes, she pushed the box away from her and dropped her head into her hands, wracked by sobs.

"Why can't I bring you back?" she wailed. "I can bring back the geranium, so why can't I bring you back?"

It took her more than an hour to pull herself together and return the box to the top of the wardrobe. Back in the kitchen, wiping her eyes, she realised she was no longer hungry. She went into the lounge and turned on the TV for company. She sat and stared at it, not seeing it, lost in thought.

I'll go to the library tomorrow.

No, I won't.

Yes, I will.

I'll go to the library and see if they have any books on magic.

That's absolutely ridiculous. I must be losing it. I'm losing my mind at last.

In the end she decided she would not go to the library tomorrow. She would go shopping instead. She would treat herself to some new clothes. She would get on with her life.

The following day, instead of buying new clothes, Martha found herself in the library searching amongst shelves of books on magic and witchcraft. All the books seemed trivial and lightweight, not what she was looking for at all. *This is silly. All those years I thought I was losing my mind, and now I really have gone and lost it!*

She had resolved to go home, when by chance she opened a thick volume she had not yet looked at. It was full of tiny, tightly packed writing that made her vision swim and etchings of witch trials that made her feel nauseated. She was about to close the book and return it to the shelf when something fell to the floor. Looking down, she saw a business card by her feet. Replacing the book, she crouched and picked up the card, reading what was written on it.

MYSTIC MISTS SHOPPE: ENCHANTED WARES FOR ENLIGHTENED SOULS.

Below this was an address in the city and various drawn symbols.

Martha held the card for some time, staring at it.

Enlightened souls? She was an enlightened soul. At least, she tried to be. She wanted to be. If she went to this shop and told them what she wanted to do, would they think she was crazy? Tucking the business card into her purse, she turned and walked out of the library.

The shop was situated some distance from the main drag, half way along a side street occupied by the mixed aromas of kebab house kitchens, urine, and the earthy smell of dripping decay. It had been difficult for Martha to locate. The weathered shop sign bore a faded but just discernible painted design that incorporated a pentagram and circular motifs just like the design on the business card. The windows of the shop had a layer of grime and, on the inside, chicken wire; the goods on display could only be viewed from outside the shop as vague and puzzling shadows. Martha found this both off-putting and intriguing.

Entering cautiously, she took in the piles of yellowing books, the ornaments, the wooden boxes and caskets, the antique cabinets, the potions in bottles and jars, the necklaces and amulets strung from the ceiling. Then, with a start, she noticed a woman sitting at a counter at one end of the shop. She was about Martha's age, but had long white hair and skin almost as white. Her face was thin with prominent cheekbones and strange green cat-like eyes. She was dressed in a loose purple velvet gown, and various oddments on cords and silver chains were strung around her neck.

"Can I help you...Martha?" the woman asked.

"You know my name?" Martha was stunned.

The woman smiled. "Are you interested in magic?"

"I...I was just browsing."

Martha crept closer to the counter, and said in a voice that was almost a whisper, "I was looking for a spell. I want to bring the dead back to life."

"Ah," said the woman. She gazed at Martha for a long moment. Just when Martha thought the shopkeeper was going to laugh out loud, instead she said, "A resurrection spell."

"Is there such a thing?"

"Of course. I have one here somewhere."

Martha felt her heart leap up as the woman began opening the yellowed books and flicking through them.

In time the woman casually said, "Here's one."

"I never thought...seriously?" Martha reached for the book.

"That'll be £150.00." The woman smiled. "For the book and another £60.00 for the spell's the ingredients."

"That's quite expensive. I...will it work?"

"The only way you can find that out," the woman smiled, "is to try it."

Martha paid for the book and left the shop. It had begun to rain. She ducked her neck into her collar and shielded the book by tucking it under her sweater.

She existed the alley and the streets were busy with traffic and glinting wetly from a downpour . People were tucked under umbrellas. Martha smiled as she walked along, despite having just spent all of her grocery money for the month on the book and the small pouch of ingredients.

The next day was a Tuesday. Martha went alone to the cemetery and found the grave of Arthur Collingwood. It was hard not to go straight to her son's grave and cast the spell over it, but she was not yet brave enough to do that. Besides, she had promised Mrs Collingwood she would bring Arthur back first, hadn't she? She stood next to Arthur's grave, and took the little cloth sack from her handbag. *This is crazy.*

She looked around to see if anyone was watching. A man passed, walking his dog. He gave Martha an odd look. She waited until he was gone then, feeling foolish, she took the items from the cloth sack just as she had been instructed to and tossed them one by one onto the grave of Arthur Collingwood. Quickly, she recited the short spell she had committed to memory and waited.

And waited.

There was a high wind in the alder trees, but nothing else. Feeling downcast, she stared at the grave. What had she expected, really? A hand up through the earth? Arthur clawing his way out of the ground, dressed in his best Sunday suit? How ridiculous! How could she have been so silly? All that money! *A resurrection spell?*

Disgusted with herself, she turned from the grave and moved along the path toward the gates. Tears sprung up in her eyes. Had she honestly thought that this would work? Did she really think that she would ever hold her baby again? *What madness!* When would she finally accept that he was dead and gone and nothing she could ever do could change that?

That evening, as she was preparing her dinner, the phone rang. Putting the receiver to her ear, it took her a moment to recognise the voice of Mrs Collingwood. She couldn't recall giving the old woman her number.

"What did you *do*?" Mrs Collingwood said. She sounded elated.

A sudden rush of emotions almost knocked Martha off her feet. She felt overwhelmed by excitement, horror, joy and dread all mixed together.

"Do? I...did something?"

"We were only talking the other day! And now he's back. Just strolled up to the front door and rang the bell. Good as new! What did you *do*, Martha? How could this happen?"

"You haven't...been drinking, have you, Mrs Collingwood?"

"Why, you cheeky young pup! Just admit it, you did something, didn't you? You did something to bring him back to me?"

Unsure what she should say or do, Martha replaced the phone on the cradle, silencing the voice on the other end. For a long time she stood deep in thought. Mrs Collingwood hadn't sounded unhappy. She had sounded overjoyed, in fact. Could it be true, then? Had Arthur returned to her? Good as new? Not like a zombie or anything like that, but good as new!

The spell had worked. The spell had *worked!* A huge grin spread across Martha's face. She felt like someone had turned on a light inside her. Or as if she had swallowed the sun.

The next day she returned to the cemetery. It was a Wednesday, although in her excitement she didn't know what day it was. Mrs Collingwood was waiting by the gates.

"Mrs Collingwood? But I thought...you said..."

"I'm so happy," Mrs Collingwood said. "Going to get your Owen back now, are you?"

"But why've you come here? If Arthur is..." She glanced around. "At home?"

"I wanted to thank you. I don't know what you could have done, but I wanted to thank you."

"I promised, didn't I?" Martha said. She was moving away, keen to get on with the task she had come here to carry out.

"I suppose you did. Now I've got my Arthur back. The only thing that makes me sad is..."

"What?" Martha said, halting in her tracks. She turned back and looked at the old woman. "What is it?"

"Well," Mrs Collingwood said thoughtfully. "It's just that now I'll have to mourn him all over again."

"Mourn him? What do you mean?"

"Well, he's going to shuffle off again at some point, isn't he, dear? He's bound to. And I'll have to do my mourning all over again, and it was so very difficult the first time."

"You?" Martha felt a shock of cold ice pass through her body.

"Anyway," Mrs Collingwood said. "You go and do what you need to do. Don't let me hold you up. How many are you going to bring back, dear? Not the whole cemetery, surely?"

"I...no...I..."

"Best of luck. You've made me so happy, you really have!"

The old woman stepped forward, clutched one of Martha's hands in her own, and squeezed it. Then she began to walk away. Martha was rooted to the spot, staring after Mrs. Collingwood. She thought about the time when she had lost her son. All those months of pain and weeping. All those years of mourning.

"No," she said, to no one now. "I can't. I can't do it. Not again. I just...couldn't."

Reaching into her pocket, almost without thinking, she took out the little cloth sack and tossed it into a nearby litter bin.

To her son's grave she took only flowers, and a few final tears.

Everybody Needs One

David Elliott

CYNTHIA HAD BEEN appearing in wet dreams from the age of twenty-one. She was young. She needed the money. And for centuries, for millennia, she'd prospered. Her profession, one of the oldest in the dream world, was much sought after. Life was good, business was good, and Cynthia was feeling fine.

But that was before the imagination recession. Afterwards, things had been very different.

There had been a downturn in imagination for many years, especially when it came to Cynthia's particular area of expertise. Wet dreams had been the most secure of all dreams at one point, the basic human desire for sexual fulfilment not being easily quashed, but with the invention of the camera, the magazine, the dirty movie, and, the final nail in the coffin, the internet, adolescents boys were using her services less and less, spoiled for choice as to the various ways of satisfying themselves during their waking hours.

Wet dreams were going out of fashion. They were old hat, obsolete. They were so last century.

'Extra in a nightmare? Me?' Cynthia walked down the Boulevard of Broken Dreams, taking a left onto Shattered Illusions Avenue. She kicked out at a stray, black, dream cat. 'I don't do extra work, thank you very much. I was the Queen of the wet dream, for God's sake!'

She hated the dream-job centre. It was so demeaning. But what could she do? She was redundant. When the waking world had unlimited pornography at its fingertips, why should they tax their imaginations? She'd been sat in the centre all morning, hoping against hope that they'd find something worthy of her talents. And what had she been offered? Health and Safety Assistant for 'Falling' dreams, Crowd Member for 'Naked in Public' dreams, Post-dream Cleaner for 'Teeth Falling Out' dreams. And, finally, the insult of all insults: nightmare work. The lowest of the low. And not even a starring role. Extra. Nightmare extra.

She was Cynthia Sex-Kitten McCoy. A star, not an extra.

And then she had an idea.

Imagination was in recession, sex dreams were obsolete, but money dreams, dreams of wealth, possessions, power, these were more popular than ever. Cynthia came to a halt, started to retrace her steps, came to a junction, and took a right into Vanity Street. If the Jobcentre couldn't help her, then maybe the dream world's foremost cosmetic surgeon could.

'You want to look like what, Miss McCoy?'

'Money, Doctor Faustus. I want to look like a million dollars,' she said, before adding: 'Literally.'

'I see.' The Doctor adjusted his glasses, fiddled with some pens in his breast pocket, and looked generally nervous. 'So you want me to transform your entire body into rectangular pieces of green paper?'

'Yes, please. Piles and piles of the stuff.'

'I see.' The Doctor started to massage his temples. 'And are you one hundred percent sure about this, Miss McCoy? I hope you realise that if you change your mind, it'll be very difficult, maybe impossible, to return your body to its current configuration.'

'I won't be having any changes of heart, Doctor. Don't worry.' Cynthia let out a broad smile, the first for several years. 'I won't have the time.'

When Cynthia first saw herself after the operation, she wasn't subject to any kind of shock. The sight that greeted her when she looked in the mirror was so unlike the body she'd grown accustomed to that it was hard to even recognise it as herself. In place of the human-like body, was a floating collection of paper money, green, crisp, wrinkled, specifically positioned to suggest actual body parts: a head, four limbs, several piles of bills to form a torso. None of these parts of her new anatomy were actually joined, each simply levitated, hanging in mid-air, drawn to the others by some mysterious magnetism. More bills crisscrossed her, orbited her, danced around her constantly.

Doctor Faustus had even provided two coins for her eyes.

'It's perfect,' she said. 'I love it.'

That night, Cynthia launched herself into a new sphere of dreaming.

The first few subconscious minds to latch onto her essence, to draw her in,

were plagued by worry. Where's the next meal coming from? How will I ever pay those overdue bills? Minds that were reaching out for her, screaming for a respite, in dreams, from the stress of day-to-day living. Cynthia spent a fair portion of the night feeling quite positive about things. This new occupation was turning out to be quite rewarding. For one night, at least, she could arrive in their dreams, soothe their worries, albeit temporarily, and leave them ready to face the trials and tribulations of the waking world.

And then she felt it. An inverted gale of suction, pulling her away from the people who needed her. Cynthia recognised the sensation at once. She'd been very familiar with it during her past existence. Need was a strong force, that was for sure, but not half as strong as Want.

Want pulled, Want sucked, Want wouldn't stop until it was satisfied.

The first of Want's subjects was Jeremy Goodwin, a stockbroker from central London. In his dream he threw Cynthia down onto the bed, ripped her apart, writhed around in her, completely naked, before exciting himself so much that he was forced to wake up with a cry of ecstasy.

The second servant of Want was Sinead Baxter, the director of a number of retail companies in Manhattan. Sinead dragged Cynthia into the bathroom of her penthouse apartment, threw her into the Jacuzzi, squeezed her until green liquid money seeped from every banknote. Sinead removed her clothes, stepped into the Jacuzzi, rubbing her naked body with notes, submerging herself in the bubbling green water, even drinking the water.

But Want had no intention of letting Cynthia hang around. Her next stop was the mind of Alan Horseman, a property developer from Sydney. Upon entering his subconscious, Cynthia found herself separated into various piles, each pile on a plate. The jowls of Alan, the several chins of Alan, were hanging about her. He was sweating with the effort of picking up a fork, of sticking the fork into a pile of Cynthia. And he was drooling; thick strands of saliva dripping from his lips, beads of sweat dripping from his face within a face. Mouthful by horrific mouthful, he consumed Cynthia, chewing her, sucking her, devouring her, swallowing her, digesting her. He had two forks now, was eating with both hands.

And then, sweet merciful God of dreams, she was leaving. Want was calling her once more. 'No.' It was no more than whisper, an unheard plea as she plummeted through the dream world. 'No more, please. No more.'

And then, blackness, stillness, quiet. She could no longer feel the obscene pull of Want, could no longer sense the futile tug of Need. Could this be the place she'd heard so much about from other dream artists? The place between Need and Want? Was Cynthia actually in the fabled realm of Nothing? If so, it was certainly a depressing place to be.

She started to move again, but slowly this time, leaving the embrace of the silent dark, being gently pulled in a new direction. There was nothing selfish about this attraction; no degree of Want was involved. It was Need, Cynthia was positive about that, but it was a Need deeply buried in the dreamer's subconscious, a Need that had been aggressively denied, securely locked away, boxes within boxes. This Need was immense, dwarfing even the towering levels of Want she'd thus far experienced. But it was weak, its strength drained by decade upon decade of neglect.

And, Cynthia realised with horror, her body was starting to change. She was moving faster now, the Need growing in strength. It had awaked for the first time in decades. It was hungry. And what was it doing to her body; the beautiful crisp green body she'd been given by Doctor Faustus? On the other hand, did she really care? This body had brought her nothing but grief, and so perhaps it was best to let the Need have its way with her. Need, after all, could never be as profane as Want. She could feel herself shrinking, growing fatter, a layer of fur growing over every surface.

But why? What on earth did it want?

Let it go, she thought. Whatever it is, it can't be as bad as being rolled in, bathed in, drunk and eaten.

And so she did. Cynthia let it go, let herself go, closed her eyes, and gave into the increasing force of Need.

Cynthia opened her eyes soon enough to see the Houses of Parliament, to hear Big Ben chiming the hour, before she was whisked into a packed House of Commons. She flew past the Prime Minister's face (who was in full flight, shouting at the leader of the opposition and making several off-colour remarks about his Mother), took a sharp right, and barely had time to recognise the face of the Chancellor of the Exchequer, taking a mid-day nap, before she was deposited deep within his subconscious.

It was dark in there. Dark and scary.

Cynthia immediately conjured up a circle of light. And, more importantly, a mirror. She was keen to find out what a person could need so deeply, that they could completely transform the shape of an experienced dream artist. The mirror arrived, as did the light, and Cynthia almost choked on her own revelation.

What, in the name of sanity ...

A Teddy Bear?

Yes, Cynthia was a Teddy Bear; soft brown fur, big blue eyes, the kind of bear any child would be happy to call their own. What was going on? This was the Chancellor of the Exchequer, a man responsible for some of the most unpleasant budgets of recent times; budgets that preyed on the weak, the poor, the disabled. Could the blackness in his soul really be explained by the lack of that one essential childhood thing?

Did the Chancellor of the Exchequer really just need a Teddy Bear?

Cynthia stood looking into the mirror for quite some time, examining her new body, patting her round fluffy belly, squeezing her furry new ears. She could get used to being a Teddy Bear, she decided. It was certainly a lot more wholesome than her money idea. People weren't likely to perform the lewd acts she'd experienced that night with a Teddy Bear. Were they? Well, even if they were there couldn't be that many of them.

With a brief flash of inspiration, Cynthia suddenly saw her future mapped out. There would be a great deal of self-sacrifice involved, like all truly charitable acts, but she was prepared to suffer. After all, how else could she hope to help so many, purely by taking up residency in the dreams of one man?

There was no question about it. Cynthia knew what she needed to do.

'And, furthermore,' said the Chancellor, 'I would like to apologise for last year's budget. I'm not quite sure what came over me. If the people of Britain would be good enough to forgive me, I assure you it'll never happen again.'

The Prime Minister was mortified. He stared at the back of his Chancellor's head, mouth agape, from the front row of the Commons, mentally willing him to keel over: Heart attack, stroke, aneurysm, anything would do. This was not what they had discussed, this was not the plan, this was a fucking disaster.

On the other side of the house, the members of the opposition were even more flabbergasted. Here was a man that represented everything that was bad about his political party, coming out with a budget plan that made their own manifesto look positively right wing. Higher tax for higher earners, tax breaks for the working class, extra funding for the NHS, University fees abolished, free ice cream on the last Thursday of every month. It was as if an alien from the Planet Nice had invaded the Chancellor's body.

'I realise there are many out there who may hate me with a passion,' he went on. 'I'm sure that to some, if not most of you, the very idea of giving me a second chance makes your stomachs turn. But, as Fluffy quite rightly pointed out, if I don't at least ask you, the British people, to forgive me, if I don't beg you to forgive me, then how will I ever know?' He stepped back from the box, knelt on the floor, and looked up into the nearest TV camera. 'Forgive me,' he said, a single tear coursing its way down his cheek. 'Please forgive me.'

And that was all it took for the unusual silence in the commons to be broken. The intrinsic horror of an MP asking for forgiveness, of acting like some kind of servant to the general population, was enough to cause uproar. Members on both sides of the house rose from their seats, shouting at the Chancellor, jeering at him, arguing amongst themselves, filing towards the exit. They were in shock, every last one of them. And the Prime Minister, who had not yet moved from his seat or moved his lower jaw back to its original position, seemed unable to do anything but watch his kneeling, begging Chancellor, wishing every kind of tragedy under the sun to fall upon him, hating the very air molecules that surrounded him, and trying to make sense of the one word, the one name that was running through his fevered mind.

Fluffy, he thought. Fluffy, fluffy, fluffy, fluffy ...

Who was this Fluffy who had been advising the Chancellor? Some old Etonion chum? A member of the opposition, detecting the early signs of the Chancellor's obvious nervous breakdown and taking advantage? He would find out, by God. He would find out, and make them suffer.

Fluffy couldn't remember a time when she wasn't a Teddy Bear. She knew that there had been such a time, but it was a hazy, practically non-existent memory. And that was fine. She was happy in her work.

She snuggled in close to the dream child, let him pull the duvet over both of them. In his dream, the Chancellor of the Exchequer was three years old. He couldn't remember a time when he didn't have a Teddy Bear. Fluffy had always been there for him, and always would be.

He loved Fluffy. He was a happy child.

Tanked

Beau Johnson

MY FATHER STARES at me, bubbles rising from his nose. I tap the glass and conclude that the soul must exist once the body has died. His head sits there, the thick black hair he's always had momentarily waving in accordance to my tap upon the tank. His eyes are open and they freak me out; so much so that I turn my wife. "Can we do it doggy-style? Him looking at us is starting to get to me."

"Sure," she says, and we finish in-between the coffee table and couch.

My mother is the one who wanted him in the fish tank. Said a prick like him deserved no better. "He can sleep with the fishes," she'd said, and then laughed that queer laugh of hers; always too high, always too long. Poor soul, my mom: even in her dreams her dreams won't come true.

"Why doesn't he decompose?" In all fairness, it was a relevant question.

"I don't know. Maybe evil is beyond ending." Sarah looked at me from the counter, came over and poured me another cup of coffee.

"Do you think he still sees?"

And that was how my wife and I started fucking in a room which now held the head of a man who'd ruled in absolutes. Sarah—she is the craziest woman I know. Not insane crazy, just, you know, a little weirder than most. She knew about my father, his organization, and the way I'd been raised. This didn't bother her, not in the least. Most times this made me smile. Sometimes though—sometimes we all need a little alone time to let out the air.

You gonna mind me, boy. It wasn't a question, not really, but it made its way into my day quite often. It was the tone which accompanied the saying, however. To Anthony Carmichael, tone was everything.

I wasn't the only one who took the brunt of my namesake. I was specific, yes, but so was my mother, each of us a pet project to my father's special ways. I concede my mother's life has been worse than mine, her going through things I will never know about—things she would choose to never tell. In my books this makes her my favourite, looney-tunes or otherwise.

"Come on, let's do it right in front of him. Let's pretend he can see." So we did, there at the beginning before we knew he was still alive; Sarah on her knees, me within her mouth. If I remember correctly, her cheek at times touched the glass. This is when I noticed the bubbles. No biggie, I thought, just left over air. When I noticed the glare, and then the deepening of his brow....

"How?"

I couldn't answer her, not outright. I thought of things though...things that go around and come around; of fathers and mothers and sons; of life and death and rage. And then I thought of the shots he had been taking. The ones he never missed. Might be a scam, sure, my father had said, but what the fuck, we only live once, right? Whose it gonna hurt?

We laughed as I remembered this, though Sarah far harder than I. Her exact words being: wow, hypocrite much?

And so now we sit, sometimes a cloth over the tank, sometimes not. Sometimes we feed the fish, sometimes we have to go out and buy more. I will not lie: it makes me happy either way. Happy he is unable to judge and happy I can finally make him see; that he can only ever watch me now, at my choosing, a man who is the complete and utter opposite of everything he stood for.

For so long I had sought his approval. This even though he was the way he was. I often believed this made me weak, he the most obvious reason for my doubt. But we are given two parents. Most of us anyway, and I am supremely fortunate for such an event. I see that now, my mother half off her rocker notwithstanding. In truth, I am glad he pushed her as far as he did; that finally there came a time where she could be pushed no further. I imagine it came as quite a surprise to my father that he went out the way that he did, and by the same signature he chose when taking out rivals. That the man was made, that we are made, is what makes it all the sweeter.

"We can start trying to have a child now, then?"

At this I realise how perfect my wife is; she's there inside my head. She smiles as I enter her, but I only see this because of the reflection from the glass. I pump. I pound. I thrust. My father watching this all from his side of the tank. Done, I concentrate on his bubbles. That and, of course, his glare.

Going Nowhere

Michael McGlade

BRENA RUSHED TO meet the flotilla as they thrustered onto the planet's surface in a weeping of red dust. When this gritty cough settled she was standing next to *Going Nowhere*, her husband's hover boat.

Damy clambered down and Brena was leaning into the catchment tank, having fumbled it open, a charred-electric reek off the rusted hull. Inside a vast black emptiness. Brena's stomach growled and the echo reverberated like some wetly black apex predator on the prowl. Times were tough and getting tougher. Never easier.

"You didn't get nothing," she said.

"I got some."

Damy upended a sack and onto the dirt fell something not even a cat would hairball, a twisted mess of wires and seared plastic and space rocks.

In days of old the men's gravity nets used to bully asteroids to the planet surface and had salvaged derelict cargo ships, abandoned fighters, even a marine core vessel that had unfortunately been stripped of everything except its hull, which now housed their church—prayers might not have delivered material wealth but at least none of them had died in a couple months.

She lifted a space rock and turning it over in her hand light caught the surface and she almost fainted because it was gold, liquid gold she gripped in her hands, but then the sun set and the rock was just a lumpy rock again. Worthless.

"What about the particle traps?"

"You'd have heard the klaxon had there been anything caught. Did you hear it?"

She chewed her lip, then gathered the gnarled and twisted filaments, the copper spools coiled like grass snakes, and went off without glancing back. Mars—having provided for her mother and mother's mother, back and back—now there was only this.

Inside this marine core vessel's hull, upturned with its deck on the ground and keel knifing the sky, the congregation bellowed a hymn and Father Nezal scrubbed the altar with incense, hunched over and stiffly stooped for as long as Brena could remember him. When she collected communion wafer in her mouth she stared at those hands of his, curled like sea shells. A wonder he could still perform.

Back in their pews and on their knees the entire village, not more than a hundred of them, waited for the blessing to leave. Father Nezal wearing a brown robe that must have been white once, maybe a decade ago, studied their gaunt faces, these coughing, spluttering, wheezing survivors.

"Patience," he said. "Grant us the patience to await better times."

Brena had made fists and didn't realize until Damy placed his hands on hers, swallowing them in his meaty, callused palms.

"*The Others* will return for us. As promised. They're exploring new regions for us to live, but they'll be back. When they departed, eight years ago, they asked us to remain strong and keep the faith. One day they will return for us."

A fire in the old priest's eyes now.

"We have faith in the old ways. We will be ready. When generations ago we were forced to abandon Earth to come to Mars, it was the sky provided our bounty, saved us, brought us here, and when *the others* departed for Titan, it was space provided their safe passage."

A murmur of agreement.

"Technology brought us here, and it will rescue us. We must capture better derelicts ships, ones with serviceable technology so that we may salvage it and build the machinery to survive until *the others* return."

A cascade of applause.

"Space provides what we need until then. The tides of our Mother Galaxy shall provide."

Brena bit her lip and blood bubbled onto her chin. Demy kissed her, taking her wasted blood into him.

Brena's inventory of survival: hooks stabs, net burns, broken bones, blisters, bruises, knife lacerations, hands worn from scrubbing, cleaning, shining until the waters she rinsed her treasures in ran red. Market preparations were everything, and she meant to get what little money there was from the vendor even if it meant her friends went without.

This particular buyer, Dr Keve, came here only because it was the cheapest place on-planet, and he erected his rickety wagon with its sides of slatted aluminum for displaying items, none of which the villagers could ever afford to purchase. They came to sell, at any price.

Gently, gently, gently Brena placed her treasures on the velvet inspection mat.

Four gold credits for the lot.

"Five," she said.

Keve grinned, teeth with more gold than her life was worth.

"Brena, you'll be the death of me."

He swept her treasures into a crate and indicated for the next in line.

"What news?" she asked. "Outpost Two, they are still in drought?"

"Made a huge haul last week," he said. "Best I've seen in years. Might be you can trade them your water, they've the credits for it now."

"Southern siders always get the good hauls. Not like us."

Brena and Damy ate silently and wolfishly, and the food was gone in moments. Soup and hard bread. She had a crumb remaining and split it with her husband, needed him strong.

"Gravity net is fried," he said. "Had a good run with it... Maybe there's a few trawls left in it, probably less."

"Can we borrow the parts we need?"

"No one has them to spare."

"What happens when it's broke—we starve? Like the Rossons. Like the Coxands. Like the Ryantes." Her cheeks had flamed the high red colour of the planet surface. "They wasted away and no one helped. No one has anything to give. Just melted away into dust. That's all Mars is—dust and bone. It'll be our bones next to feed it. It wants us. Not be happy till it gets us."

"We'll survive. I know it. When *the others* left, we survived. No one thought we'd last, but we did."

She laid her head on the table, surface rough from when she chiseled it out of the solid bedrock.

"The villagers will help us," Damy said. "They like us. They'll have to help."

She brushed the worn animal hide off and rolled onto her side in bed. Damy was breathing regularly, eyes shut.

"What it would take to get off-world?" she asked.

"Shush now."

"Catch the right ship in your net, we could get out of here."

Damy sat and studied her face.

"Don't talk like that," he snapped. "Don't ever again let me hear you talk like that."

She curled into a ball.

"*The others* said they'd be back for us, back from Titan when the colony was secured. They said for us to wait right here for them, and here we'll wait."

"What if they don't come back?"

He moved beside her, taking her in his arms, wrapping round her like an octopus on its stony mount. She relaxed, stretching out in his unwavering embrace.

She said, "Tomorrow will be a better day."

Had always said it.

Always.

From the dock Brena studied the boats buffeting at near-space casting their gravity nets, toiling to snare something of value. Brena held her breath and got to fifty before her lungs burned, then she kicked around a pebble in the dirt, bullying it, making it dance. Holding her breath was agony. She'd been holding her breath all her life. Waiting.

It was time for the boats to return. Brena stood at her chosen location and *Going Nowhere* landed inches away, the thrusters scorching her brick red. The women in the hangar applauded. How she had never been crushed...

Damy came down and the other men surrounded him. Brena forced her way to the centre of the circle and there was Damy with something unique and *weird*. A treasure. It was a curved blade, fat like a teardrop, with a green stock the distinctive patina of aged copper. Men's hands were groping for it but Brena snatched it clear and clutched it to her chest. The men stared at her and she backed up to her husband, the men's eyes penetrating, regarding her like a piece of meat.

Then she felt the sting. She'd cut her hand. That's what they were staring at, the blood. The faintest touch of the knife blade on her hand had been enough to open a wound. Out there for eons in darkest space and still it cut her. Like it wanted blood.

"Scrap," Damy said and the men brayed laughter. "Pretty scrap but scrap nonetheless. Still, might get us something other than soup and stone bread."

When everybody else had gone, Brena approached Dr Keve's market stall. She placed her treasures on the inspection mat: a cluster of copper mesh, three siderites of decent quality iron, fragments of laser-fizzed titanium, and the knife.

He lifted the blade and turned it over in his hands, face a stone stare of pure awe. Looked like he'd never let it go again. She snatched at the blade but he danced backwards, clutching it to his chest.

Rounding the inspection table, she approached him, warily.

"Name your price."

"Not for sale," she said.

He moved backwards until he ran out of space and then he lurched for the driver's seat of his wagon. But she was on him, her hands pincering for the knife, and they tussled, tumbling to the dirt. She clung onto the knife like a barnacle, wouldn't let it go, not dare allow him to steal her treasure. He slapped her face and slapped her again, her head juddering like a struck bell.

The dirt grew red, clotted, blood cascading from the neck wound. Brena stood, legs tremulous and she crashed into a shelf, using it to keep from falling, and she watched Keve twitching on the ground like a decked fish, blood bubbling from the laceration to his neck, and then like a light had been switched off his eyes darkened and he was dead.

Blood all over Brena, inking like a crimson bloom on her tunic, and forbidding herself to weep she knew what had to be done.

The waters went red from scrubbing and she buried her clothes in a hole she scratched with bare hands. During dinner and later again she had tried to find the words to tell her husband what had happened, but could not. There was no forgiveness for murdering a man, then dumping his corpse and wagon in a gorge. And now laying here beside Damy in bed she shook him awake and told him to be still for she had something—some *thing*— she must say and those earth-blue eyes of his looked on and she collapsed onto her side away from him so he couldn't see her miserableness. He took her in his powerful arms same as he had done every single night of their union, and still the words that jumbled through her mind would not escape her lips. She. Couldn't. Say.

"You'll be gone before I wake."

"Aye, same as always."

"Tomorrow will be a better day."

The boats returned with the greatest single day haul ever. Damy drew out a cup, a plate and a band of twisted gold that fitted Brena's upper arm like it had been tailored and the pattern on this gold band spiraled outwards like a seashell and her gaze drew down into it until she stumbled and almost fell and lurching backwards from the crowd of gleeful scavengers Brena glanced upwards at the sky which too spiraled outwards into infinity, onwards and forever, and she bent double, slow breathing to stop from sicking up.

"We're saved," Athet said. "Saved. The sky provides."

And a cheer went up.

Brena clutched the knife which she had secreted in the waistband beneath her tunic, and the blade was warm to touch, pulsing like it contained breath.

The next day's haul was good but not as great as the previous, and the following was fine, and the next adequate, and then the hauls faded to rocks and fragments, same as it had been before.

The knife in Brena's hand glinted in the bruised evening sun that slatted through the church windows. Alone, for she had sought much isolation since the murder, she clutched the fat blade to her chest. It was icy, searing her hand with its chill, but she held it tightly, drawing it closer to her breast. This was all the riches she had ever dreamed of.

Father Nezal sat next to her on the pew and studied the object clutched to her bosom.

"God has never before gifted us such wealth."

"Not *God*—the sky."

"God, sky they are the same. What matters is that people *believe*. Faith is what has keep us alive these long years. Faith and blood."

Holding the blade, she knew what must be done. What else did they have to trade ... except blood.

Everybody had gathered in the village center and when Brena held the blade aloft silence ensued. There had been a heated discussion about the death of Dr Keve but the sight of the blade brought them to a moment of introspection.

"It's the only way," Brena said. "Or we can starve slowly again."

"It can't be true," Athet said, one of the eldest and most respected women. "If we do *this*, take lives, then we don't deserve to live."

Pockets of arguments broke out and in the mayhem Father Nezal rushed Brena and grabbed the blade. They struggled, rolling in the dirt, and the priest yelled and snarled and whimpered, kicking back from her, his hand bleeding. He'd cut himself on the blade and not by accident: Brena cut him purposely. Everybody had seen it.

The klaxons shrieked, announcing the particle traps had been sprung, and instinctually the men rushed off to their boats, for at any time, day or night, once the traps were sprung they'd set off to inspect them.

Before long, the men returned and displayed nuggets of purest gold. Enough to feed the village for a year.

"It is a trick," Father Nezal said.

"No, it's blood," Brena said. "Blood is what we need. Get it and we'll have enough to build castles, to get ships, to leave if we want but why would we want to leave Mars when we have everything we've ever wanted here."

And the crowd took Brena onto their shoulders, hands grasping and prodding and caressing her like a holy relic, and Father Nezal, hunched over and infirm, hobbled off into the church.

He was a sickly young thing, not much more than bone, and had made the miscalculation of stopping over in the village on his way to an outpost. Laying in bed with his eyes shut, he did not hear them enter his room. Brena made the incision at the artery in his neck and by the time his eyes sprung open his blood had spurted onto the bed sheets and he was dead.

"Why do you think no one ever comes here?"

The church was empty and had been so for weeks.

"Because they're fools," Father Nezal said.

"I'm not talking about church," Brena said. "I mean *here*—Mars?"

He was sitting on a chair on the altar and Brena was kneeling at the foot of an idol she herself had carved from granite.

"None of our race has ever landed on Mars, not since *the others* went away," she said. "Because we've been left behind. We're the failures. The sick and the weak. We were abandoned here to die out of existence."

The priest stood and lurched at her but then stumbled onto the ground and, the strength having diminished from him, he lay there, unmoving.

"Are you going to sacrifice me?"

"A man of faith? Not even I would do that."

"You must stop this madness, Brena. You started it and now you are the only one capable of stopping it. Listen to reason."

Months later, the hauls diminished. In the meantime they'd hunted and killed nine people. Now, no one came to their village any longer, certainly not by accident or happenstance. Weary travelers sensing their fate avoided the area entirely.

Instead, Brena and her followers turned their attention to the inhabitant of a village, about the size of their own, which was a day's journey off. And, having been blessed with good fortune, they had salvaged equipment such as body armour and blasters, so it was that they surrounded the village at sunup.

"Who do we take?"

Brena said, "Why not them all?"

A year passed before the hauls diminished. They had material wealth, all the gold and silver and copper they could fish with their gravity nets and magnetic beams, but still no space crafts, no interstellar apparatus, nothing that they could use to construct a vessels capable of delivering them off-planet and into the blue distant yonder of space. Getting off-planet was a necessity because what good was all the gold they'd amassed if they couldn't trade it, and there was nothing left on Mars to trade. No people or outposts or villagers or merchants or vendors to trade with. All that remained was this village and its inhabitants.

"The sky will provide," Brena said. "If we are willing to make the right sacrifice..."

She glanced at the waxy faces of her friends and neighbours, of their children, the priest, and her husband.

"Who out there is willing to give their life in order that we survive. Who will be the one to save us?"

She held aloft the blade, which gleamed like fish scales, and which never needed sharpening, that had gotten shaper with each cut. She could taste the blood of her kill, salty as seawater.

"Who will it be? Who is worthy?"

The door shattered and they were on her, pinning her to the bed, holding her immobile. She writhed and thrust with the strength of ten, but the villagers were collectively strong enough to subdue her.

"Damy, help me..."

Brena stopped resisting when she saw who had taken her knife to hand. Damy pressed the blade to his wife's throat, this simple fisherman, and the wound on her neck yawned open, red as a gill.

In Which It Goes Pop

Jeremiah Murphy

IBRAHIM NEEDED TO breathe, but this wasn't an option. It wouldn't let him. He couldn't hide either. With its six eyes and—what were those? Talons? Claws?—that could rip through any of these western Indiana trees as easily as it did his camping equipment and his right arm, the creature would find him, easily. The only thing to do was keep running.

His lungs told him otherwise. They forced him to slow to a jog, and then to a walk, and then to stop altogether. He sucked in what he accepted as the last air he'd ever enjoy and waited. Soon enough, a breeze tickled his back before rising into a gale.

That thing's claws were sharp enough that he hadn't noticed the gash in his bicep before he saw the blood, so Ibrahim hoped that whatever death it had in store for him would be just as painless. He closed his eyes and turned around.

He opened them again when someone grabbed his left hand. That someone was a black-haired woman whose curls were streaked prematurely with silver. Her dark eyes and full attention were on him as she smiled encouragingly and asked, "Want to get out of here?"

Her fashion shouldn't have been quite so annoying to him, given the circumstances, but really, an orange-sweater-vest/green-necktie/leather-messenger-bag combo was, frankly, criminal. He also felt like maybe he should warn her about the creature that was about to kill him gruesomely, but it was *right there*, and if she hadn't noticed yet, that was her problem.

It roared.

With the palm that wasn't wrapped around his, she blew a thick, gray cloud as if it were a kiss.

The roar became a howl of pain and confusion.

She pulled Ibrahim away and ran. He managed to keep up by following the hope she carried with her. After a minute or so, she looked over her shoulder dragged them to a halt, announcing, "We should have a little bit of time before it can pull itself together and come after us."

"What?" he stammered.

"That?" she asked, taking a moment to examine his arm. "Powdered graphite. Air and earth are natural enemies, so something as quintessentially ..." She frowned for the word and finally just gave up. "Earthy? Earthen? Anyway, it's disoriented, but not for long."

When it came to confusion, Ibrahim sympathized completely with the creature. Self-preservation had kept him from questioning anything so far. But now he began to process this sequence of events, and they baffled him so much he hardly noticed her ripping up his sleeves to bandage his injury.

"The good news is," she told him, "you'll live. The bad news is, we're going to have to get you to the hospital if you're going to want to stay that way. Where's your car?"

Finally, something he knew the answer to. He pointed.

She removed from her pocket the kind of brass watch on a chain that old-timey, rich people used to wear. When she popped it open, though, it turned out to be a compass, with a tightly rolled up scrap of paper where the needle should be. She studied it, muttering, "And ... the monster is ..." She snapped it closed and nodded in the direction of his car. "That way. Of course the monster is that way."

Now that his pulse simmered down a little, Ibrahim could finally spit out the thing that had been bothering him since this morning. "*What the hell was that*?"

She strained awkwardly to reach into one of the side pockets of her cargo pants. "I told you: graphite."

He blinked.

She straightened up sheepishly. "Right," she said. "Sorry. That was a kamaitachi, a Japanese wind spirit, or a wind demon; the distinction is a little blurry over there. Anyway, it shouldn't be here in the Midwest—or in this world, really—so I need to send it home."

"It's ferrets!" he exploded.

"Weasels, actually."

"Three flying weasels with swords for arms!"

Her eyes lit up, and she grinned. "I know!" she squealed with far more delight than seemed appropriate.

He sputtered, "Is this *fun* to you?"

"Of course not!" she replied. "Maybe. No! Okay, a little bit."

"It's trying to kill us!"

"Yeah, but you said it yourself: it's three flying weasels with swords for arms!"

"What the hell is wrong with you!"

"Don't worry," she told him, showing off what she'd retrieved from her pants, "I'm sure I have this under control."

"That's an egg."

"And this," she added, "is a golf pencil."

As she scribbled some strange symbol on its shell, he asked, "Why are you carrying an egg in your pocket?"

"Because I never know when I might run into a kamaitachi," she replied. "Kidding. I never thought I'd ever see one of these before I died. Time to write that on my bucket list and cross it off, I guess."

"But ...?"

"When I hit it with this, the proteins inside will temporarily bond with the spirit's—or demon's, whatever—corporeal form, and the breaking of this sigil will disperse with its ethereal side, banishing it. I think." With an embarrassed shrug, she admitted, "Come to think of it, I probably should have opened with this." She held her free hand out to him and raised her eyebrow. "Shall we?"

They crept in the direction of his car, his ears straining for the slightest clue that three flying weasels with swords for arms might be near. And sure enough, after they'd covered about half the distance, a breeze picked up.

"Get behind me," she told him.

He had no problem with that.

The kamaitachi approached, angry and strangely adorable.

"Are you positive about this?" he whispered.

She grinned, turned, and tossed the egg. It smashed into a tree at least a meter from any of the weasels that made up the monster. "I should have brought more eggs," she muttered.

The kamaitachi charged.

"Run for your life!" she ordered, and Ibrahim obeyed.

He made it all the way to his car, before his culturally masculine brain flooded his lizard brain, questioning his worth. How could he leave this person alone, with that ... thing? Sure she knew what it was, and she was confident she could stop it, but what kind of man would abandon a woman like that?

He turned back and saw nothing but a cloud of dust and leaves, from which could be heard growls, hisses, thumps, and the occasional human yelp. Suddenly, a pop and a flash of light filled the forest, and when it passed, it took with it both the kamaitachi and the mystery woman.

His face and shoulders fell. He never said thank you.

The air fell still, and gradually, bugs and birds resumed their conversations. He understood then that he was safe—that is, until a twig snapped behind him. He whimpered and nearly fell over, until a pair of human hands caught him and straightened him out.

"Are you okay?" asked the mystery woman who, at the moment, was the most beautiful person he'd ever seen, despite the fact that she was now covered in glitter, confetti, and what appeared to be yogurt.

"I think so," he replied.

"You're only saying that because you've lost a lot of blood, and your endorphins are blocking out the pain. I should probably drive." She cleared her throat. "I mean, can I have a ride? I left my van in Terre Haute, and there's a hospital there."

"Yes, please," he mumbled.

"Thanks!" She kissed him on the cheek. "I meant to tell you, I'm Rafaela. Torres. Rafaela Torres. I never caught your name."

Ibrahim fainted.

The last thing he heard was her voice. "That's okay," it said, "you can tell me later."

The Man in the House in the Sea

Andrew MacKenzie

I BUILT THIS house and I live in it. There is no phone here, or television. There is electricity, in the form of a petroleum-powered generator, which allows light, heat, and refrigeration for certain foodstuffs. The house appears old due to weathering caused by salt spray from the sea—in which the house is located.

During low tide the house is accessible from the shoreline by way of a raised wooden walkway I also constructed. During high tide the sea obscures this walkway and renders the house inaccessible, as the construction intended.

The shoreline is grey and jagged, and does not attract many people, though what people do make their way there often stay to observe this house. Some cross the walkway and knock at my door. They leave when they receive no answer.

For the moment the tide is down, and there is a couple on the beach. They have noticed the house, and are taking pictures. It is a cold day, and windier than usual; they will not linger. I make my way to the kitchen and prepare a light lunch. When I return to the window the couple is gone. The shoreline is empty and the sky is overcast and grey, though I make out the exhaust trail of an aeroplane flying west overland. I finish my meal and return to the kitchen to brew tea, which I hold with both hands next to the living room window. The glass is scalding hot. The shoreline is empty and the sea washes against it. I drink deeply.

The house sways and creaks with the movement of the sea and wind, constantly. I am seated now, and the sunlight is fading. Soon the tide will be high enough to obscure the walkway. Though the placement of the house, combined with the movement of the waves, makes swimming here from the mainland difficult, it is not impossible.

It is darker now. I can no longer hear the water break against the walkway. The tide is high. After turning on the kitchen light I stand by the window. Now that the water no longer washes against the hollow walkway, the hum of the generator is audible. A faint glow remains along the horizon; it allows me to make out the shoreline still. I watch until the mainland becomes a black shape against the sky. The wind has calmed and the sea is no longer rough. It would be easier for someone to swim, now, despite the darkness, as the house would act as a bright beacon. I open the window and push my head out. I hear the generator and the slow creaking of the house, only. The generator is located across the hall. After I decide to turn it off, I return to the living room to listen. Would I be able to hear the splashing and heavy breathing of a swimmer? If so at what distance would they become noticeable, one hundred meters? Ten? With the generator off the house is dark, but the moon is visible tonight, and bright. The swimmer could also use the walkway as a guide, underwater though it may be, it would still be easy to locate, resting just a few feet below the surface. Therefore leaving the house in darkness would not deter a swimmer, and would only place myself at a disadvantage.

After turning the generator back on, I turn on the lights in every room. This illuminates the surrounding sea. I stand next to the bedroom window, which I have opened. A vantage point on the second floor affords me a greater sightline, and a better grasp of sound as the humming of the generator is muffled. I watch the sea, and listen.

I am becoming too tired to remain vigilant, and I consider checking the locks on the doors and windows, securing the nightly barricades, and sleeping. As I turn from the window however, I hear them, the swimmer. A jagged breath, perhaps, I hear it, perhaps fifty meters away. They must have lost control of their breathing, or mistimed a stroke. It will be a costly mistake.

The circle of light seems to be growing smaller; the sea is soaking it up greedily. I can hear it, sucking up the light into blackness. The house creaks loudly. I have seen the swimmer; the sea has been unable to prevent that, three times at least, skirting the edge of the light. The distance must be too great for them to swim underwater, so they bide their time, waiting for me to tire.

The sun will be rising soon; already it illuminates the water and the edges of the shoreline. I see the dim shape of the swimmer retreating to the mainland. It flickers indistinctly, which suggests they are swimming underwater much of the way, to avoid being seen. But I see them. I saw them.

The sun is rising and there is no need for the lights. I turn them off. It takes a long time to traverse all of the rooms. The tide has lowered and the walkway is now visible. I feel no need to secure the barricades. I stand by the living room window and watch the sun rise fully. The stairs seem intimidating in my weariness, so I lie on the couch.

When I awake it is late afternoon, and I am hungry. While I eat a light lunch I stand by the living room window and watch the shoreline. There are several people walking along the shore, and all of them are taking pictures, some of the house. The wind is calm, and there are fewer clouds, a day more suited for these travellers and inquisitive photographers. I draw the blinds mostly closed, and brew some tea. The glass is scalding hot. I can see the shoreline through the opening of the blinds. I drink deeply.

So There I Was

Michael S Walker

"SO THERE I was..."

Will had to grin as he continued his seemingly interminable walk toward his ten AM job interview. It was something Aaron, his friend in California, liked to repeat ad-nauseum when he was shit faced. High-concept joke. Sounded like the start of an extremely long but interesting anecdote. "So there I was, searching for Livingstone in the jungles of Africa, when all of the sudden a Bengal tiger leaped out of nowhere..." "So there I was, collecting moon rocks on the moon, when all of the sudden a naked moon maiden leaped out of a crater and proceeded to..." The deal was that Aaron never said anything at all after the preface, just left the audience hanging. "So there I was..." he would begin brightly, looking down in glazed wonderment at his Xth beer. He would then smack his lips and nod his head, as if he were replaying in his mind the amazing story he was about to relay. But there would be no story. Aaron would just hoist his beer and take another long swig. And then, maybe fifteen minutes later, he would say it again, to the annoyance of everyone else.

"So there I was..."

"So there I was, in industrial park hell," Will said, as he continued to walk around the perimeter of a squat glass building, searching for Suite 103A and the spacious offices of Spiritual Changes. He was beginning to be a bit concerned because he had been around the building twice now (this was the start of his third go round) and the company in question just did not seem to exist. There did not seem to be a Suite 103 A. At least not on this building. There was a Suite 103, but the company housed there was called *Analog To Digital High Concepts* or something like that. Not Spiritual Changes. All of the company names were embossed in bright white letters on the black glass of the office doors: Analog To Digital High Concepts...Creative Data Matrix Analysts Incorporated...Specter 8 Survey And Investment Group...All sorts of bullshit titles sounding like Mafia front companies. But no Spiritual Changes. Absolutely not.

It was possible that Will had copied down the wrong address, or was on the wrong street entirely. For the millionth time since leaving the house that morning, he looked at the torn envelope on which he had scrawled all the info the manager of the company had relayed to him over the phone yesterday. Her name was Sandra Coping. He had committed that name to memory. The business was called Spiritual Changes, a small, mostly state-based company that helped clients make changes in their lives through the use of hypnotherapy, relaxation therapy, exercise, music...Sounded like a bunch of new-age crap to Will, but he was in desperate need of a job. Any kind of job. It was a desk job, the impossibly perky Sandra Coping had told him over the phone: scheduling clients for appointments, taking care of correspondences and faxes, answering the phones. Basic administration. The pay was eight dollars an hour. And the address was 1039 Woerhle Road, Suite 103 A. Yes, it was possible he had copied the address wrong. But Ms Coping had repeated it twice. And she had a very pleasant and clear speaking voice, one of those voices that sounded to Will like a happy robot straight out of the Stepford Wives.

"No I have to be in the wrong place," Will thought, as he completed his third circuit of the impenetrable glass building. The site could have been some ancient temple from Atlantis. Besides the cars and SUVs gathering heat in the parking lot, there were no signs of habitation or human life for that matter. Just obsidian glass and phony sounding names.

"So there I was..." Will whispered with a sigh, as he sat down on the sidewalk that skirted the building and considered his slim options.

From one of the front pockets of his black slacks he extracted his cell, annoyed as always at the tiny blue display and the tiny little frosted letters that proclaimed immediately: NO SERVICE. Of course there was no service. You had to pay the bill in order to have service, and since Will had been forced this month to choose between paying the bill or covering the rent, he had wisely opted for the latter. He had been amazed though at how swiftly the company had turned off the phone. Four days after the due date on the bill he had been trying to make a phone call to his wife Mattie. He had been downtown seeing about a secretarial position with (of all places) the Church of Scientology, and he had missed the No. 2 bus. Since it was Mattie's lunch hour at the middle school where she worked as a secretary he had hoped she might swing by with the car and take him home. But as soon as he had dialled the number, a pleasant-sounding woman (perhaps the phone sister of Sandra Coping) had come on the line and said : "We're sorry...we cannot complete this call at this time. Your service has been disrupted because your phone bill is now past due. If you would like to resolve this issue immediately, please press 1 and we will transfer you to the next representative..." Well of course, Will would have liked nothing better than to have resolved the issue immediately, and the bill was only two-hundred dollars, but it was two-hundred dollars that was not to be parted with at the time. Will still had no idea when it was going to get paid. Maybe after he found a goddamn position somewhere. Anyway, he carried the phone with him as a digital watch these days.

Will flipped the phone open to check on the time. 9:46. If he didn't find this place soon, he was going to miss the job interview and then have to take the bus home.

Will sat on the stoop in front of the hated office building and studied the picture of his wife Mattie, which was the wallpaper on his useless little cell. For a second he felt a tiny bit better. He didn't deserve someone as beautiful as Mattie, Will thought, studying his wife's shy smile, her plump rosy cheeks, the hazel eyes that seemed to shine perpetually with amusement and yes.

"Don't know what I'd do without you, darlin'" Will whispered, nodding his head and closing his eyes.

Abruptly, he shut the phone and stood up, automatically dusting off his dress slacks as he did so. He looked west in the direction he had come from. It was about eight blocks back to the bus stop. Did he just want to forget about this whole thing and head back that way? Will wasn't even sure if there would be a bus through any time soon. He wasn't familiar with this bus route at all. It was the Number 98, or, as it was sometimes called, the "Zoo Bus" because the last stop on the line was the metropolitan zoo. Will didn't know if a return bus came through with any frequency or if, as was the case with some of the routes, there were only a few morning and evening runs.

Next, Will looked east. Behind a row of twisted, tiny trees with bleached-out green leaves was yet another glass building—the twin of the building he was standing in front of. (Perhaps Spiritual Changes was housed in that building?). Beyond that was a giant green corrugated structure, perhaps a warehouse of some kind. There was a well-manicured lawn in front of this building, on which three or four industrial sprinklers were now sending forth great arcs of cool-looking water. On the other side of the road, a vast cornfield stretched off toward the east—a great square of imposing-looking cornstalks.

"Fuck it," Will said. "Go east young man." Will figured that if he did not come across the doors of Spiritual Changes (which was beginning to look more and more likely) at least there was a chance of coming out on a main road somewhere and getting a bite to eat in a Bob Evans or something. Most certainly he would be able to find a pay phone, call the Columbus Transit Authority, find out what bus he needed to hook up with to get home. There was absolutely nothing like that west, in the direction of Dudley Road and the bus stop. Just an overpass and a large exclusive-looking golf course, the Gulliver Country Club or something like that. Will had been very amused by the name and, as he walked past it, had had a fleeting image of the hero from Gulliver's Travels striding the links like some imperturbable Colossus, while tiny Lilliputians in plaid golf pants tried to drive away from him in carts suddenly the size of white ants. That had been diverting for about five minutes or so.

Will now walked away from the glass building he had been orbiting. He walked across the parking lot and over a small grass divider, to the next squat glass building and its front of tiny ugly trees. They were very unusual looking trees, only about seven or eight feet in height, with dark, furrowed trunks. Will wondered what kind of trees they were. For someone with a BA in English, he was surprisingly ignorant of things in the real world.

Just to make sure, Will started to circle around this building as well, reading the signs on the office doors. No. No Spiritual Changes here either. Bundo Restaurant Fixtures and Appliance Store... Fiber Optic Solutions...The Carlyle Paper Mill...More empty-sounding names. Each office was just a dark door flanked by two equally inscrutable windows. Will was half-tempted to go into one of these places, see if anyone knew where the elusive Spiritual Changes office was. But for some reason, he refrained. He just made a single orbit around this building, and then walked over a grassy knoll and out to the berm of the road. He continued east.

"Yeah...I'll just find a Bob Evans...get a bowl of soup or something," he said, as he began to walk toward the green warehouse and its oasis of sprinklers.

As he walked, a maddening procession of cars sped past him, kicking up little wakes of dust and hot air. Will tugged at the collar of his too-tight white shirt, at his black tie, at the lapels of his gray suit jacket, wishing he could just tear off the whole formal straight-jacket and walk down the busy street semi-nude. But no, that was not an option. In his hand he clutched the envelope with the address of Spiritual Changes, the bus route info, and a copy of his resume and references. All of these were beginning to get a little wrinkled.

Will noticed there was a THIRD glass building, sitting far back from the main road, at a halfway point between the second building and the green warehouse. He thought for a second about walking back to it and seeing if Spiritual Changes leaped out, but then he decided against it. He took a quick look at his cell-phone watch. It was 10:30 already. He was just going to let this one go, start again in the morning. He hadn't really been that keen on working for a bunch of new-age quacks anyways.

He thought, with a sigh, of how Mattie would react when he got home and told her he hadn't been able to find the place. She would grill him of course about his attempts to discover it.

"Are you sure you checked ALL the buildings?" she would say. "Maybe you were on the wrong side of the street...?" Will dearly loved his wife. She had always been supportive of him in their six years of marriage. But things had been slightly strained since Will had lost his job teaching English composition at the Kelso Charter School in Dublin, particularly in the last few weeks. He wasn't that keen on doing anything else really, and his reluctance to interview for jobs he thought beneath him was beginning to frustrate his usually low-key wife.

"I really should check over there too," Will sighed, reconsidering the third glass building, which sat about a block or so back from Woerhle Road. He didn't want Mattie to think he hadn't tried.

This building was not the home of Spiritual Changes either. Once again, Will resolutely walked around the structure, examining the doors, unloosening his tie as he did so. The building was absolutely identical to the other two he had inspected, except for one minor difference. There were no company names embossed on any of the narrow doors. Instead, there were only numbers. 1,2,3,4...the sequence went all the way up to 16 and then Will found himself back at door number 1 and the beginning of the building.

"Do you, Will Corburn, want what's behind door number 1, or do you want to go for the fabulous green warehouse that's down the road?" Will said, in his best imitation of a game show host. Maybe the heat was finally getting to him.

Will decided, before he moved off, to try one of the glass doors. His curiosity was piqued. Did any of the denizens of this industrial park hell know where the fabled Spiritual Changes was? Did it really exist?

Will settled on door number 2. He tried to open it, but there didn't seem to be any handle on the door—just the large white NO. 2 in the very center of the glass, and a keylock on the frame at the left. Will got very close to the dark glass, brought his hands up to the sides of his face like blinders, and tried to peer into the office or whatever it was. He might as well have been peering into a crater on the moon.

"Hello?" Will said, feeling extremely foolish. "Hello? Is there anyone in there?" He wrapped against the door several times, stinging his knuckles in the process.

"Owww..." he said. "Shit..."

For a second, Will though he heard something—a slight rustling sound, as if someone was moving a stack of papers around on a desk. And then, Will's heart stopped in his chest when this tiny noise was followed by the loudest crash he had ever heard. It sounded as if two cars had collided with each other behind the glass door of the office. Either that, or someone had managed to upend twenty or so filing cabinets all at the same time.

"What the fuck!" Will shouted, jumping back a foot or so from the door and staring at it as if he had just discovered the entrance to the seventh circle of hell.

Nothing else happened. Complete silence behind door number 2. No after shocks. No sounds of embarrassed or apologetic employees. Nothing but the steady wash of cars on Woerhle Road as they went east and west.

Will stood there, his heart now hammering in his chest. What the HELL could have made all that racket? He was afraid to knock on the door again for fear that such an action would precipitate yet another explosion.

"Everything OK in there?" Will managed to croak. God, he was getting dehydrated. I need to get somewhere and get a drink, he thought. Or anywhere. Anywhere but here. This building, with its numbers and its inexplicable noises was making him very nervous indeed.

"OK then," he said, stupidly. "Thanks..I'll be going then...if everything is OK?" He turned tail then, barely restraining himself from bolting toward the green warehouse and points beyond. He managed a brisk walk away from the glass building. As he did so, he thought he heard the paper rustling start again behind No. 2.

Will went to the very berm of the road, and walked on toward the green warehouse with its three moving arches of silver water. He wanted nothing more now then to get out of this damn place. He took off his tie all together and stuffed it in his jacket pocket. Cars continued to fly past him like some kind of Chinese automobile torture.

"What the hell was that noise?" Will said out loud. The place was really beginning to overwhelm him—the sterile-looking buildings; the nonstop onslaught of traffic; the heat, which seemed to be rising by torturous increments. The weatherman on Channel 4 had said today was going to be a scorcher. He had not been lying at all. And, to the best Of Will's recollection, he had not seen a single living soul since stepping on to Woerhle Road. He tried to look through the windshields of the oncoming cars, get a glimpse of the drivers, but the windshields seem impenetrable as the glass of the buildings he had just left behind. He finally just put his head down and continued to walk.

"Spiritual Changes, my ass." Will said, as he trudged onward, trying to shout out the blitzkrieg of traffic and heat. On the curb, at Will's feet, were a number of orange trident symbols, spray-painted there at intervals of about a foot or so. Bright orange tridents pointing the direction east. Will assumed the tridents marked water lines or gas lines. Something else he was not too certain about.

Will checked his cell phone again for the third time. 10:28. How time flies when you are NOT having fun. Will wished that the damn cell worked, that he and Mattie had been able to scrape together enough money to pay the bill. He could give her a call right now and report to her how shitty his day was turning out to be. It would just have to wait until he found a working pay phone.

He continued walking, following the orange tridents as if they were street signs or something. The grass at his feet was, for the most part, dead—almost white. Only up where the sprinklers were raining was the grass sleek and green and pastoral looking.

"Take me down to Paradise City, where the grass is green and the girls are pretty...Oh please, take me home..." Another bit of business inherited from his alcoholic friend Aaron who, when he was really inebriated, would eschew the "So there I was," bit to sing the Guns and Roses song in a toneless, whiny falsetto.

Will glanced over to his left. Sitting back, even further from the road then the three glass buildings, was a strange hybrid of a structure. He hadn't been able to see it at all before. The top three stories of the building were glass and steel, almost resembling the buildings he had left behind. The rest of the structure was brick, ornate, almost gothic in structure. It looked as if a skyscraper had been dropped down on a hundred-year old church. There was an archway in the center of this eccentric structure and two words were etched in stone above this archway: "Central Office." To one side of the Central Office, a metal tower stood like some kind of abstract religious icon. High-tension wires crowned this structure, running north and south. The whole bizarre assemblage was ensconced behind a high fence that did not seem to have a gate or any other entrance as far as Will could tell. He stopped to stare at it for a minute. He could hear the high-tension wires buzzing, like the sound of advancing insects.

"So *that's* the Cental Office," Will said, trying to joke. "Curiouser and curiouser..."

Will stood and stared at the building for several minutes: at the slivers of white clouds that were reflected in the upper glass panels, at the giant black crows who hopped around uneasily on the impenetrable fence, like dark sentries. The building made him feel, well, disturbed... Once again, he took out his cell phone. He aimed the small camera lens on the phone's lid at the structure and took a picture of it for posterity's sake.

"Mattie will never believe I saw somethin' like this," he muttered. When he was done taking the picture, he checked the camera function on the phone to see how it had turned out.

"What the fuck?" he said, looking at the picture he had just snapped. But it was not in color at all. It looked very much like some photographic negative. There was the strange building—basically a glowing white blob behind the imprint of what was now a black fence.

"Damnit, if there is something wrong with this camera..." Quickly he aimed the phone at the green warehouse, snapped the shutter again. No. No problem with the camera. There was the warehouse on the viewer, it's color a little washed out because of the low pixel quality of the camera. But it appeared very normal.

Will mopped at his brow. What the hell was going on here?

"I don't know...don't want to know..." he said, and one of the black crows on the fence cawed at him in agreement.

Rather than save the picture of the Central Office, he deleted it from his phone and started walking again, picking up his pace as if he were some power walker in a mall. He removed his suit jacket and draped it over his sweating shoulder.

"The sooner the better...Take me down to Paradise City, where the grass is green and the girls are pretty...Oh, won't you please take me home..."

The traffic continued to blow past him. Some of the cars seemed intent on running him over; they got so close to him as they passed by. He tried, once again, to peer past the windshields, catch a glimpse of someone else in this industrial park hell but he could see nothing. He inched away from the berm of the road, and just concentrated on the walk ahead.

He wished, vainly, that he knew the area better, what roads up ahead intersected with Woerhle Road, but he was an idiot when it came to directions. He was constantly amazing Mattie with his inability to get from point A to point B.

"All I know is I'm headin' for a big glass of somethin' cool," he said, smacking his lips.

He reached the area of land on which the green warehouse was situated, with its powerful sprinklers. It really did feel like some oasis in a vast desert. It even felt as if it were a couple of degrees cooler. Very carefully, he started to skirt around the first of the sprinklers, which automatically sent a jet of water in a southward arc, from close to the base of the building to a few inches beyond the berm of the building. He walked around the dark stain of water left on the road, being very careful that no traffic was bearing down on him as he did so. He felt very tempted to run into the spray of the sprinkler and cool off even more. That would be wonderful.

"You'll be OK. Just jeep walkin', Corburn," he said to himself. He skirted around the stain left by the second jet of water. As he did so, he stared into the arc of the sprinkler as it watered the warehouse lawn. A rainbow appeared in the drops of water—a tiny little arch of ghostly colors. His eyes focused on it, and everything else seemed to melt away for one perfect second...

A car horn jolted him out of his reverie. Automatically, he stepped back, away from the curb. A yellow truck had come out of nowhere, almost running him down.

"Damn it, watch where the fuck you are going, asshole!" he shouted at the receding truck. God, this day was proving to be an absolute waste of time. He could not wait to get off Woerhle Road.

As he stood there, glaring at the truck, he was greeted with a downpour of water. In his anger at almost being run over, he had totally forgotten about the sprinklers in front of the warehouse.

"Shit!" he yelled. Now he was both angry and wet.

Curiously, the water from the industrial sprinkler did nothing to make him feel any cooler. Where the water had touched his head and skin (he was wearing a short-sleeve shirt) he felt a strange electric tingling. It was almost comparable to the feeling he used to get on his tongue when he was a kid and he pressed the poles of a 9-volt battery to it. His skin seemed to be buzzing. It was not a pleasant sensation at all.

"What the hell now?" Will said, rubbing at his wet skin. He felt dizzy. What is going on here?"

He stumbled out to the road and skirted carefully around the last sprinkler. Walking made him feel a tiny bit better. But his skin was still stinging. And there were black specks swimming across his eyes. The heat was unbearable.

"Mattie.."he gasped. "Mattie..."

Will Corbun suddenly found himself standing in front of the same glass building he had been standing in front of forty minutes before. There could be absolutely no doubt about it. There was the same glass door with the legend: Analog to Digital High Concepts. There was the identical glass building next to it. And there, now in the distance, was the green warehouse Will was certain he had, only a few seconds before, been standing directly in front of.

As he had earlier, Will sat down on the sidewalk. Or perhaps it would be more accurate to say that Will's legs gave out underneath him and he fell to the sidewalk.

Will did not say anything for two or three minutes. He just sat there, dazed, looking west and east, his mouth open, his breathing ragged.

"Umm..." he started, but he could think of absolutely nothing to say after that. He reached into his pocket and took out his cell phone again, opened it up to look at his wife's face on the screen. At least that was still there.

"Mattie," he said. "Mattie...Mattie...I don't think...I don't think we are in Kansas anymore..."

Slowly, Will Corburn's mind started to work rationally again. It didn't seem possible but there it was. He had somehow, by some extraordinary means, been pulled backward instantaneously a quarter of a mile or so, almost to the very beginning of Woerhle Road. He looked at the door behind him. There could be no mistake. It was Analog To Digital High Concepts. It was Suite 103. It was the same glass building. By some fantastic trick, it was the same glass building he had started out from.

"Industrial park hell," Will croaked. "I am in industrial park hell. And there doesn't seem to be...any way out..."

Will snapped his cell phone shut, stuffed it back in his dress slacks. He let the papers he had been clutching all morning (still damp from the sprinklers) fall out of his hand and lay there on the pavement. The only direction he wanted was away from this place. Away...Away...

"Will Corburn got up, not dusting off his pants this time, and walked back to the door labeled *Analog To Digital High Concepts.* He didn't even try to open the door. He just started to beat furiously on the glass.

"Hey...open up in there!" he yelled. His voice sounded completely ragged. "Is there anybody in there! Open up...!"

He beat on the door for about a minute or so and then, once again, put his hands up to the sides of his face and tried to peer through the glass. Nothing. He could see nothing.

"Hey, open up!" he yelled again, beating on the glass as if he were trying to shatter it with his fists.

Suddenly, Will was aware that the cell phone in his pocket, a phone that hadn't worked for two weeks now, was ringing. Right before the phone had been disconnected, Will had disconnected the Ramones' "Blitzkrieg Bop" as a ringtone for the phone. The song was now playing, muffled by the pocket of his pants.

Once again, he pulled the phone out of his pocket, annoyed. Who could it be, except the phone company reminding him of his unpaid bill? Well, he would tell them...

He flipped the phone open, held it to his ear.

"Yeah...what?" he said.

A tiny blast of bright music jabbed Will's ear, and then a man started talking. His voice was deep and sonorous, almost creepy.

"Will Corburn...you have reached the offices of Analog to Digital High Concepts...We are not here right now. In fact we are never hear right now. So please...stop knocking on our door..."

Will dropped his cell phone. It fell on the pavement with a clack. The voice continued talking but he could not hear what it said. His wife's smiling face stared up at him from the open phone.

Will left the phone on the pavement. He ran, in a panic, away from the glass office building and out to Woerhle Road. It was a miracle that he was not hit by a car. He continued to run across the road and into the green cornfield on the opposite side. He plunged into that dense square and continued to run, the leaves of the plants slapping at his body. He had absolutely no idea where he was going, nor could he really see where he was going. All he knew was that he had to get away...get away...from Industrial Park Hell.

Will ran. He lost all sense of time. He ran until he was breathless, flailing at the corn in front of him, trampling it down with his feet. He ran, with sweat running down his forehead, stinging his eyes, making him blind.

Suddenly, he was aware that he had come out somewhere. There was another road in front of him, traffic barrelling up and down both lanes.

"Help!" he croaked, waving his right arm at the oncoming cars. No one paid him any mind at all. He was suddenly aware that he had lost his good suit jacket somewhere during his plunge through the expanse of corn.

Across the busy street, there were several buildings. Will had been dimly aware of them when he had emerged from the field, but he had been so intent on trying to stop someone that they had not fully registered in his mind. Now, he glanced at them in horror and realized where he was...

They were the very same office buildings he had left behind. There could be no doubt. He was right back where he had started from...

Industrial Park Hell

Industrial Park Hell

Industrial Park Hell

Will started to run...

"So, do you have any questions for me?"

Will shook his head. Where was he? He seemed to be sitting down, not running. At his right side, a woman, dressed elegantly in a sharp gray suit, was peering at him over a brown clipboard. She had large, brown eyes, a thin tanned face. She was in her late thirties or so. In her right hand, she had a ballpoint pen poised inches away from the clipboard. She seemed to be waiting for Will to say something.

"I'm sorry..." Will said, glancing around the room. He realized that his voice was back.

"I said, do you have any questions for me...about the job?"

The room was a square painted completely white. A large desk ran from one wall almost to where the woman was sitting—one of its sides almost touched her knees.

"Job?" Will said, stupidly. He was still trying to comprehend what was going on. The last thing he remembered was the cornfield. Starting to run across Woerhle Road...the glass office buildings...dropping his cell phone...losing his suit jacket...no escape...

He looked at the woman.

"Anything at all?" she asked, nervously.

The woman's voice sounded very familiar to him. Who was she? Did he know her? Then it came to him. It was the voice of the woman he had talked to on the telephone yesterday. He was certain of it. This was the director of Spiritual Changes. This woman was Sandra Coping. He glanced at the desk and was rewarded with confirmation of this. There was a small gold plaque sitting at the edge of the desk that read: Sandra Coping—Director of Operations.

"No..." he said, slowly. "I really don't have any questions...about the job..."

"Well," Sandra Coping said, writing busily on the clipboard. "In that case...if you have no questions...thank you for coming in and seeing us. We'll let you know...if you have the position." She stood up, placed the clipboard and pen on her desk. Will stood up as well. He was suddenly aware that he was once again wearing his suit jacket, that his black tie was noosed tightly around his neck. Was he suffering a breakdown? He didn't remember meeting this woman. He didn't remember sitting through any sort of job interview at all. All he could remember was walking on Woerhle Road. Being lost on Woerhle Road. Not being able to escape from Industrial Park Hell. That was all. And now...

"Thank you," Will said, wanting to say something. He stuck out his hand, and Ms. Sandra Coping reluctantly shook it.

"Have a nice day," she said, ushering him out of the spartan office, through a hallway, and into a waiting room of some kind. Plastic chairs flanked one narrow plywood wall. There was some kind of reception area to Will's right—a counter, and behind that a small desk with a computer monitor and a rolodex. Will shivered as he walked. Even with his suit jacket, it was deathly, deathly cold in the offices of Spiritual Changes.

"So once again, thank you for coming in and good luck to you," Ms. Coping said.

Will studied her face. It was absolutely impassive, unreadable. He looked into those brown eyes that seemed to be as impenetrable as...

"No problem," Will said. Was it possible he had hallucinated the whole episode? Was it possible that he had sat through an entire job interview with this woman? He could remember nothing but...

"Good luck getting out of here," Ms. Coping said. It sounded as if she were anxious for him to leave now.

"Yes," Will said. He glanced over at the desk and the computer monitor. He suddenly notice that there was a picture on the monitor, and he gasped. It was a picture of a white blob behind the imprint of a dark fence. It was the picture of the Central Office, the same picture that he had snapped with his cell-phone camera.

Moment of Time

B.M. Long

THE RED-HAIRED WOMAN stepped inside the store and headed straight toward the cash register. After greeting us, she laid a box on the counter and unwrapped a hideous bauble. I recognized one of our golden clocks. Everything in it symbolized bad taste, from the poorly painted ornamentations to the plastic imitating metal. We had received three of these, one of which had been on display in the window, so they had sold quickly despite their deplorable price to quality ratio.

The customer's timepiece did not work well. Apparently, the hands accelerated or decelerated for no reason. Hitting the pane with a nail sufficed to adjust the mechanism, but it did not last. Inserting new batteries had not solved the problem. The customer was hoping to exchange her clock, however we had run out of them; she was forced to choose something else. The defective item belonged to a low-price batch, and we could not return it to the supplier. My boss gave it to me, even though the novelty was not our style at all.

"Thanks!" I said. "Marshall is in for a surprise!"

I arrived at the house in the middle of the afternoon and placed my acquisition on the table. I set the hands to 3:15 p.m. I then started to sort pictures that had been stored in a binder for months. My niece's wedding, our vacation in Prague. Remembrances from our hotel and what we had done there flew toward me like the Vltava river under Charles bridge.

The hands showed only 3:30p.m. when Marshall came home. I jumped at him and took him to the bedroom for a timely nap. A little later, I asked him why he had been let go so early. I glanced from his puzzled look to the golden clock's pane. It had stopped. Ultimately, instead of surprising my husband, I was hoisted on my own petard. I told him the story, which gave us a good laugh.

The timepiece would have ended in the recycling if we had not invited friends over the following day. Like me, Gisele worked in a store selling decorative accessories. My husband cooked a delicious meal, we shared enthralling conversation—and the item went completely unnoticed.

When Geoffroi and Gisele left, my watch showed 11 p.m; the clock attested merely 8:30 p.m.

The night inspired in me an idea that I enacted the next morning. First, I sat in a comfortable armchair with a book by Angela Huth. How delightful! After about forty pages, I glanced at the bauble. The second hand appeared almost motionless. Indeed, I had not noticed the time passing.

Then I took an apron, vinegar, and wipes and got down to cleaning. Scrubbing the bathroom seemed to last for hours. As soon as I was done, I rushed to the living room: the hands turned at full speed.

The timepiece worked perfectly, but it represented the psychological time. What would we do with it? Would my love discover how much science fiction bored me? Would we exchange conniving glances when certain family members declared that our clock was fast? Too bad it was so ugly, I thought, as I put it away in the closet.

Minefields and Meadows

O.L. Humphries

HENRY THORNALLY LOOKED like a man with the weight of the world on his shoulders as he fumbled with the lock to his second-floor apartment. He had to give the key a vigorous wriggle before the decrepit lock's tumblers eventually clicked into place. Pushing the door open, he revealed the interior of the flat. Mary was sitting at the table, a pile of notes in front of her. A vase of daffodils stood at the far end of the table. She looked up just in time to see Henry catch his crumpled overcoat on the door handle.

"God dammit!"

There was a distinct tearing sound as Henry freed himself. If possible his already tatty coat had just become a little more so. He flung his briefcase down and kicked it with a startling degree of venom under a nearby chair. Then he wrestled his way out of the overcoat, which was promptly discarded with equal contempt onto said chair.

"Cup of tea, dear?" asked Mary, as she always asked. She got up and made herself busy around the kettle, without even waiting for a reply. "Bad day at work?"

This was the question Henry had been dreading. He plonked himself down by Mary's pile of notes and took a deep breath.

"Yes. We've had a major setback today."

Henry hated lying to Mary, although he knew she wouldn't understand the truth. Technically, though, he wasn't lying. He *had* had a major setback at work today. It just wasn't the same work Mary thought he did. Henry had been unemployed for four months now, or as he preferred to think of it, unofficially self-employed, during which time he'd been working on his own secret project. Unfortunately, Henry had recently been encountering an increasing number of setbacks. In fact more setbacks than progress.

Mary tottered back to the table with two brimming cups of tea and set them down. Then with a pitying look in her eye, she took up Henry's bedraggled overcoat and began trying to smooth some of the creases from it. "You know, you should think about getting a new jacket. This one's so scruffy." The coat seemed impervious to Mary's attempts at straightening. In the end she gave up and settled for simply folding the ungainly garment as best she could and draping it over the back of the chair.

Henry was halfway through his tea before he enquired, "How's your day been?"

Mary, who, now seated, had begun sifting through her paperwork again, looked up, a childish grin on her face. "I thought you'd never ask! I've had a really good revision session today. It's like everything's beginning to click. And," she scooped up a formal looking letter and waved it around wildly, " I've finally got an interview! For a really good school too!" Mary had been unemployed for two years now. As a teacher with nearly twenty-five years' experience, they'd expected her to easily find a new school after her previous one had made her redundant. However it turned out to be a struggle even to get an interview. Henry blamed it on the glut of 'dynamic young teaching graduates' that seemed to be pouring out of the universities. He hadn't voiced his opinion to Mary though.

In the meanwhile Mary filled her time with home study courses and completing a trickle of application forms.

It was great to finally have some good news, no matter how slight. Henry returned Mary's grin, and raised a hand. "Mrs Thornally? Mrs Thornally? Can I watch the telly please, Mrs Thornally?"

"So long as you sit quietly and don't disturb me. You are dismissed."

It was the happiest Henry had seen Mary in ages and that in turn made Henry happy. It was the briefest ray of sunshine in Henry's darkest days. But it faded all too soon. Even as he left the kitchen he began thinking about the risks he was taking, gambles that would have huge implications for both their futures. Did poor, sweet, Mary deserve such dishonesty? Money was running out, and with it any chance of success.

As Henry sank into the sofa, lit only by the flickering blue light of the TV, the weight of the world shifted back onto his shoulders once again.

He arrived at the house early the next morning. It was a rundown, detached building, completely boarded up. To the back was a wild overgrown garden. Henry had often thought the house would have made an excellent family home, except for the location. It had been built slap-bang in the middle of an industrial estate. Henry had always assumed that it had been intended for a caretaker's family. His father had bought it in the hopes that he could one day sell it on to an expanding business for a tidy profit. Maybe the land it stood on could be used as a parking lot? Unfortunately, like many of Henry's father's schemes, this never came to fruition. When Henry's father passed on, Henry, being an only child, had inherited. The house was totally un-saleable. Repulsive chemical smells, excreted by nearby factories, wafted round it. It's garden was choked by brambles and litter blown in from neighbouring sites. A thick layer of grime, which had issued from the nearby smoke stacks, coated the exterior. Flakes of the filth would often drop from it like dead skin cells, only to be quickly replaced by a fresh layer.

A few weeks after Henry's father's death, a woman from the council had come to inspect the property. She hadn't taken long to condemn the building as uninhabitable.

Now Henry put the house to use as the base for his (so far unsuccessful) experiments in universe-hopping.

His father's estate had not only provided a location for the project but also much needed cash. It was a pot of money Henry had to split between the project and day to day living. A useful buffer to cover up his unemployed status from Mary. The pot, however, wouldn't last forever. Things were getting tight.

One of the first things Henry had bought from his inheritance was a top of the range security system. In the dim light which crept through the gaps in the boarded up windows the hall looked inconspicuous enough. However, Henry knew the room was criss-crossed by an intricate web of infrared beams. Breaking one of the beams would trigger the release of a gas into the room rendering any intruders unconscious.

Henry had traversed the assault course of beams so many times now, that the complex route he had to take through the hall each day had become etched in his memory. His first two carefully measured paces were just the beginning. They were followed by side-steps, back-tracks and step-overs. At one point it was even necessary for Henry to get on all fours and crawl for a meter or so. Once he had reached the stairs Henry briskly brushed the dust from his hands and knees and continued up to the first floor.

Henry fired up the generators (the electricity had long since been cut off) in the spare room and made his way to the hopping room.

The hopping room was Henry's pride and joy. He often mused over how aesthetically pleasing the room was. Pale light glinted on the chrome of the wall-mounted units. The immersion tank took up the centre of the room, full to the rim with orange-brown contiguity fluid. A thick cluster of wires led from it to the largest of the units at the far end of the room. Henry pulled a leaver, letting electricity stream from the generators to the hopping room.

Like a rain forest at dawn the room slowly came alive. Diodes winked on and off, audible hums and ticks issued from many of the units, the room even filled with a distinctive smell as the equipment warmed up. He pulled up a chair next to the control unit.

After about three hours of augmenting, the system was ready for a test run. Henry left the hopping room only to return a few seconds later with what looked like a cross between a scuba diving suit and a coat of chain mail draped over his arm. This was the hopping suit. The suit was designed to be skin tight and highly conductive. A good item for transferring charge from the contiguity fluid to human flesh and spreading it evenly over the body.

Henry lay the suit in the immersion tank and watched with interest as the contiguity fluid gradually flooded the garment. It almost seemed as if the oily fluid was sucking the suit down to the base of the tank.

Henry retreated to the control panel and tapped a few keys. The clicking and humming from the units covering the walls increased in intensity, diodes ceased blinking, and they burned brightly from their housings. Henry waited a few seconds then flicked a switch. There was a sudden thunderous electrical crackle from the tank. Henry reacted naturally to the unexpected noise, crouching low behind a chair. Seconds passed. Then minutes. Henry gave up his cover and crept towards the tank. The fluid had turned solid, like a huge block of amber. Within the block just at the base Henry could make out a large flat cavity. The cavity was the same size and shape as the hopping suit.

The suit was nowhere to be seen.

Gingerly Henry prodded at the block—to no effect. He rested a hand on it. The surface was slightly warm to the touch. Then he rapped on it with a fist.

Suddenly the contiguity fluid returned to its previous state. Henry leapt back with a start. Ripples chased each other across the surface of the orange-brown liquid. The suit had returned.

Henry swung a clenched fist through the air and whooped with joy. Just as directly behind him an electrical fizz and pop from within a unit signalled a component burning itself out. Henry rushed to the control panel and flicked a switch to deactivate the equipment.

The suit had just travelled to one of the infinite number of universes in the multiverse.

Sitting revelling in his success, Henry became acutely aware that he'd not eaten since breakfast. It was now almost six. Time to head home.

A strange trend among suppliers of high technology was that they generally opened their shops late and closed them late. Henry nipped into his nearest one on the way home. He was a regular in the shop, probably their best customer. He told them the pieces he needed to replace, a list of exotic names, many of which didn't give the slightest inkling as to the nature of the component. Henry took a seat and waited for the assistant to gather his order.

The next day was bin day and even though he carried with him a bulging bag of slightly whiffy rubbish Henry was in high spirits. As he negotiated his way down the hallway and stairs grasping the glossy black plastic sack in one hand, his briefcase in the other and a rucksack over his shoulder Henry even mustered a tuneful whistle. Outside he deposited the rubbish sack on the pavement and checked that he was fully prepared for the day at work. Mary had been bustling about all morning and Henry hadn't had the chance to check over his previous night's purchases. In fact he'd almost been caught inspecting one of the larger components, when Mary had walked into the kitchen unexpectedly. An automatic reaction had been to slip the item into the black rubbish bag. Mary had given him a bemused look as she popped some bread into the toaster.

Now Henry had to rummage cautiously through the sack to retrieve the valuable component. This, however, did nothing to dampen his spirits. Today Henry Thornally would be the first man ever to travel between universes.

It took Henry only an hour or two to install the new parts, then a few minutes more to put on the hopping suit. He also donned a ridged helmet made from a material similar to that of the suit. Henry considered the helmet a particularly important item. Both the suit and helmet were designed to reduce particle slippage. Henry figured that when he hopped there was a chance some of the molecules in his body may be displaced either internally or externally to his body. So long as the slippage wasn't too large he'd be ok. Unless it happened within his brain. Just a few molecules of brain matter being displaced could potentially result in any number of psychological issues arising, loss of memory, loss of sight, character change, he could even end up being reduced to a vegetable. Hence the rather ungainly, but none the less necessary, head attire.

Henry also carried with him a water tight bag containing his clothes. This was so that once he'd hopped he'd have dry clothes to change into.

As he clambered into the immersion tank Henry felt like a piece of battered chicken being dipped in sweet and sour sauce. He slid into a lying position, bag of clothes wedged under his knees, his helmeted head the only part of his body above the fluid.

The timer had been set for 120 seconds. Henry watched the seconds slowly tick away. The suit was now completely saturated in the slightly chilly contiguity fluid. With ten seconds left Henry took one last gulp of breath and ducked down, completely submerged in the orange-brown fluid.

The counter ticked down to zero. There was an electrical crackle.

The transition was almost impalpable.

Henry's head emerged spluttering from the liquid. Bulbous droplets of contiguity fluid raced each other round the rim of the hopping helmet, merging, eventually reaching great enough mass to plummet one by one back into the immersion tank. Henry took in his surroundings.

He was in an identical hopping room, which was no surprise to him. Every universe he jumped to had to have a hopping room for him to arrive in and depart from. This meant that whatever universe he was in it couldn't vary too wildly from his own one. What he was really interested in was which universe *this* hopping room was in.

Henry scrambled from the tank, sending contiguity fluid lapping up its sides and over the rim. The hopping suit clung to his skin. He could feel liquid slowly draining from it to pool on the floor. He also became aware that the cool air was already beginning to give him goose bumps.

He peered from a window. Immediately he started noticing subtle differences. The house was still in an industrial estate. However, there seemed to be less litter, the sky seemed clearer. Hell, he could even hear distant birdsong.

Henry quickly got changed and left the house. He soon found that the layout of his new universe was much the same as his own. Most roads and buildings remained in the same positions. But there seemed to be slight variations. Had that alley been there before? Were there more houses in that terrace? The people he saw seemed happier, more content with their lot, Henry even greeted one or two of them with a cheery "Hello!" as he strolled through a park heading for the town centre. A number of times he even had his hail returned. If Henry remembered correctly, in his own universe this park was notorious for muggings, drug dealers and other seedy activities. He took a look around. It was beautiful. The grass was a lush green, thrushes and sparrows flitted from branch to branch of the elm trees that lined the paths. The sun beamed down.

The town centre in his own universe was a place Henry did his best to avoid. A haven for slack-jawed, baseball capped, oiks; spending their last few pennies in the multitude of crap merchants that lined the streets, wolfing down fist-fulls of greasy chips in between drags on pungent cigarettes and issuing expletives.

Fag. Chips. "Fuck off Darren." Fag. "You 'aint havin' none of my ciggies." Chips. Fag. "I need 'em don't I? They help me keep the weight off." Chips. Chips. Fag. Chips. “Arsehole." Fag.

The town centre had changed.

Every window display seemed to beckon to Henry. "Look what we've got," they whispered to him. "There's even more inside. Come on in."

The range of goods on display was mind-blowing: huge chocolate dripping cakes, TVs the size or your hand or the size of a wall, stereos that could blast the latest hits at you from every conceivable angle, scantily clad mannequins in the most beautiful clothes Henry had ever laid eyes on, books on every conceivable topic. The list went on. None of the crud he was used to being peddled. None of the tat that would fall apart after its first use or fail to live up to its promises. In every shop, contented customers. Behind every counter a smiling face.

Henry was drawn into a men's clothes shop. The interior was breath-taking. Rail upon rail of shirts, trousers, jackets and shoes all of the highest quality. Henry became aware that his mouth had actually begun watering as he strolled through the Aladdin's cave of clothing. Quarter of an hour later and he'd accumulated a small mountain of garments to try on. Then he found the jacket. It was the most handsome item of clothing he'd ever seen. He grasped it with shaking hands and hurried to the fitting rooms.

Quickly relegating his other selections to the floor along with his own tired coat, Henry held the jacket up for inspection. It was a deep blue-green. The colour of the sea off some idyllic Mediterranean beach.

Metallic buttons at collar and cuff were stamped with an exotic insignia giving the garment an almost military look. The fabric was tough, rugged. But after slipping it on Henry found the lining was silky smooth.

Looking in the mirror, Henry's gaze was returned by the vision of a man who knew where he was going, a man people would listen to, a go-getter, a success. Henry had to have the jacket. He rummaged through his pockets. All he had was change. Would any of his cards work in this universe? Probably not. He stared at the mirror. T he jacketed man stared back. He didn't look like the kind of person who worried about such things.

A grin slowly spread across Henry's face.

He'd just discovered an interesting attribute of the multiverse and the ability to visit any universe within it. Assuming the theory that there are an infinite number of universes within the multiverse holds true, would one crime in an infinite number of crimes make any difference? One divided by infinity is as close to zero as makes no difference. So, no. Except in this universe. Then he needn't come to this particular universe ever again—he had, after all, an infinite number of universes to visit. So, what effect would stealing this particularly handsome jacket have? Will it have an adverse effect on him? No. Will it have any repercussions for society as a whole? None he'd have to endure. Will he have a lovely new jacket? Yes.

He picked up his grubby old coat from the floor and put it on over the new one. The bulky coat easily covered the jacket. His heart was racing as he left the fitting rooms. He handed the other clothes to the assistant by the fitting room door with a curt "thank you" and headed out of the shop.

Suddenly the air was cut by the shrill sound of alarms. The jacket was tagged. Henry began running.

He wound randomly down streets and alleys. Passers-by stopped momentarily to stare after him. Someone shouted the obligatory "Run Forrest!" Henry, grinning maniacally, waved a hand in acknowledgement as he rocketed past.

A man can only run for so long in mid-summer whilst wearing two jackets. Gasping for breath, and sweating profusely, Henry ground to a halt and ducked into a narrow side street. Leaning with his back against a wall, between gulps of air and spluttering coughs, Henry began laughing.

It took about five minutes for him to regain his composure. His old coat now lay discarded on the ground.

Henry was now gasping for a drink. So, bolstered by his new found freedom, he stopped by a newsagent's; remerging seconds later with a can of cola, a chocolate bar, and a short, rather irate, newsagent chasing after him. Henry had heard that in an emergency virtually anything could be used as a weapon. So he turned and jabbed his twix in the direction of the impish shopkeeper's larynx. He missed. Instead, the inexpertly wielded chocolate bar hit the man full in the mouth and disappeared therein. The whole thing. Completely wrapped. Both fingers. Henry quickly withdrew his hand. There was a stunned silence. A look of complete disbelief filled the little man's now bulging eyes. Henry's aggressor turned and staggered back into the shop.

Later that day Henry mused that he should have gone for a toblerone. Longer reach. Sharper edges.

He hurried back towards the house. Again he was aware of small differences to his own universe, least of all that his supplier of high technology was now a curry house. His most valued shop was now called *Taj Palace*. Henry shook his head with disapproval as he trotted past.

Later, back in his own universe, Mary was pottering about in the kitchen. She was looking for the colander. Henry had just travelled to a different universe, and his wife was worried about a missing kitchen utensil. Of course he hadn't told her of the hopping room yet. He still needed time to decide how to break the news. To her. And to the world. Also, although he loved her, Henry didn't think Mary would be able to understand the secrecy, the lies, why she hadn't been told from the outset. The first thing that had happened when he walked through the door was Mary complementing him on his new jacket, asking after where he'd bought it. More deceit.

In his new worlds Henry could take what he wanted, when he wanted. Do whatever he wanted to do.

In his own grim world there were so many restrictions. He had to be so careful all the time. It was like knowingly walking a minefield when only few meters away there's a beautiful meadow. But if you've put the woman you love in the minefield, maybe that's where you should be too. Besides, the end was within sight.

Over the next several weeks Henry hopped universes regularly. He was travelling further and further afield every time, his offences becoming increasingly more brazen. Crime followed crime. He'd taken to carrying a large knife with him. He found it a most useful tool for getting people to part with their property, or at least for dissuading them from pursuing him.

It was all so easy. People simply crumbled in front of him, many shopkeepers just looking on aghast as he walked out with their stock. Henry often speculated that he'd never get away with such behaviour in his own universe. People were harder there, wouldn't take any crap. But in every new universe Henry was king, free to take what he wanted, a man liberated from remorse. There were, after all, an infinite number of universes where that man still has his wallet, where that baby still had its candy.

Then one day everything went wrong.

Henry was in the process of locking up the house, when a stern voice addressed him.

"Excuse me, sir, but I wonder if you could help us."

Henry turned to find the voice belonged to a fierce-looking policewoman. She was accompanied by an equally intimidating companion.

"We've been in the area today looking for a man who closely matches your description. The person in question has committed a number of thefts over the course of the day." She indicated a bag which Henry clutched in one hand. "Do you mind if I have a look in there?"

"Not at all." Of course the bag was stuffed with stolen goods, but Henry didn't hesitate in handing it over. They couldn't arrest him for stealing from another universe!

The policewoman rummaged about in the bag. Meanwhile her companion fixed Henry with an icy glare. Eventually she pulled out a boxed camcorder.

“Do you have a receipt for this?”

Henry responded with a defiant shake of the head.

"Then I'm afraid I'm going to have to place you under arrest. You have the right to remain silent and anything you say may be used in evidence against you. Please come with us." She took a step towards Henry making to grab his arm.

Henry's impulse reaction was to draw the knife. Seeing the weapon, both officers immediately leapt back. "Oh shit!" one of them exclaimed.

Henry began fumbling with the door lock, waving the knife menacingly with his free hand.

He'd hopped a number of times today. He must have accidentally come back to one of the other universes instead of his own.

The door eventually swung open. Henry stumbled backwards into the hall, slamming and re-locking the door behind him.

After a few seconds the police officers summoned up the courage to approach the door. Peering through the filthy window they witnessed the incomprehensible. The man appeared to be performing an ungainly dance within the hallway. Twirling and leaping. Bounding. Even crawling across the dusty floor. A look of pure concentration on his face. Once he'd reached the stairs he gave a worried glance over his shoulder and proceeded to ascend.

After a brief discussion, one of the officers left the front of the house to check the rear garden, returning shortly after to report that the garden was way too choked with brambles to offer a realistic escape route. There then ensued a longer, more heated, debate. Hands were waved, radios used. Eventually, having reached a decision, the first officer began kicking at the door. Her companion, looking less than comfortable with the situation, drew his truncheon.

The wooden frame around the lock eventually gave way with a dry crack. The door flew open. Both police officers entered the building cautiously.

The first officer had drawn a canister of pepper-spray from her belt. Carefully they made their way to the foot of the stairs, meeting no resistance.

At the top of the stairs was a stark room. Completely bare, save two clapped out generators. The officers continued past it.

The next room's door was closed. However from within came a soft splashing sound; the sound of a large body entering water. They paused outside. The male officer sniffed at the air in an exaggerated motion, then silently pulled a disgusted face. There was a sickly smell issuing from inside.

On the count of three the door was flung open.

The officers charged through and almost immediately stopped dead in their tracks. The first recoiled, dropping the canister of pepper spray to the floor with a clatter, her face turning pale at the stench, whilst the second simply stood and stared in shocked amazement. The room appeared to be entirely furnished with trash. Pizza boxes, fruit boxes, every kind of conceivable food packaging decorated the walls, held in place by poorly driven nails.

Larger boxes stacked one on another seemed to function as tables or workbenches.

The vast majority of the decoration seemed to utilise curry trays. They were stapled up everywhere. Their metallic surfaces glinting in the dim light. None had been washed. Crusted-on madras and vindaloo caked them and the surfaces they were attached to. Many had been nailed up completely full, their contents spilling down the walls, pooling on piled up trash or on the floor. Some had swollen. Like puss filled blisters, as their contents began to rot, waiting for their moment to burst.

The whole room was filled with a continual static-like hiss. The sound of thousands of insects clawing their way through the filth. Cockroaches scuttled back and forth. Maggots writhed through cracks and crevices between mouldy boxes, devouring scraps of rotting food. In one corner lay a pile of bags. The bags labels read *Raj's Palace*.

Holding back his disgust, the policeman directed his horrified gaze towards the centre of the room. There rested a large, dilapidated, bathtub, full almost to the brim with rust-stained water. On its surface floated an oily film.

Within the bathtub lay the man they were pursuing. His torso wrapped in tinfoil. A colander strapped to his head.

Stool Fool

Douglas J. Ogerek

MY CRAP LOOKED like an A one night. I showed my wife. She said, "Weird. I've made lots of Is, Js, and Cs. But an A? That's unique."

"We should take a picture," I said. "Call the paper. I can see the headline: 'Honorable Discharge.'"

We laughed. Thought nothing more of it. Until the next night: I got a B.

"You've heard of alphabet soup?" she said. "Well this is alphabet poop!" We laughed.

I said, "My GPA has dropped."

"GPA?"

"Grade Poop Average."

"No matter what grade you get, it's always going to be crappy."

"And no matter what grade I get, I'm expelled." We laughed.

We chalked up the A and the B to a fluke. Shit happens, right? But if I had known those letters were the beginning of what would plunge our relationship into the toilet in less than two weeks, I never would have shown them to her.

The next day, we went out for dinner.

I said, "I dropped off a letter today."

"To whom?"

"To me, I guess."

"You wrote yourself a letter?"

"No, no. I dropped a letter in the toilet."

"Ha ha." She rolled her eyes. "What letter?"

"Oh, maybe you don't care."

"No, no. What letter is it?"

I said, "It sounds like you don't really want to know."

"Please. Just tell me."

"Guess."

"Don't tell me it's a C."

"No."

"Well, what?"

"What do you think?"

"Jerry, just tell me."

"Fine. It's an S. A-B-S. I think this could mean something. Maybe it's spelling out a longer word. Like 'absent' or 'abscond' or 'absolute.' Maybe even 'abstemiousness' or 'abstruse.'"

"How about 'absurd?' I think your A-B-S theory is just BS."

"How do you know?" I said. "You with your occasional Is and Js and Cs?"

"All of a sudden the toilet's some kind of crystal ball?" she said. "Jerry and his crystal bowl. All signs point toward a shitty future."

The next day, I thought more about what ABS might mean. Was it an acronym? Anti-lock brake system? Stop? Stop doing something? A-B-S. Was it talking about abdominal muscles? Somebody's initials? Or maybe some complex code? Maybe some message that would change my life.

When I received a T the next night, I elected not to tell my wife. A-B-S-T. BATS? STAB? Abstruse?

The following evening, I peered into the receptacle. What I saw resembled a massive boulder beginning its descent down the left side of a mountain peak. This time, I decided to show my wife. "Last night, I made a T. But I'm not so sure about this one."

"I guess that's it," she said. "Sorry. A-B-S-T. Looks like an end to your streak, except for the one at the bottom of the bowl."

After she walked away, I looked in the mirror, and what I saw in the bowl was no longer a massive boulder commencing its descent. Instead, I observed the next stage of the masterwork I was gradually unveiling, for the mirror revealed an "R."

"It's not an R," she said. "You're making a mountain out of a dunghill."

"I think that you're envious because you were incapable of interpreting the next piece of the puzzle."

"You're right. Let's see...A-B-S-T-R. Perhaps we should rearrange the letters. BRATS maybe? Or STAR then a word that starts with B. What do you think?"

STAB R is what came to mind. "Oh, I have begun to catalog my thoughts. However, my preference is to patiently await the next component."

"Let's hear your thoughts now. Maybe we can figure it out together...make a game of it!"

"This is not a game," I said.

"Oh, right. This is some serious shit. Let's tell some of our friends about it. Maybe ask my mom. Perhaps we can start a spiritual movement...travel around the world preaching the good news according to your butt."

"Our friends are far too sophomoric to even conceive of something this profound. And your mother?" I chuckled. "She got squeamish when we revealed that the mushrooms she was eating were shitake."

"Oh, right. This is a special message just for the two of us."

"We are the elite," I said. "Presently, the only ones capable of grasping its meanings. Our unequivocal calling is to interpret these works and share their philosophical implications among the elite."

"Works? So you're an artist now?" She looked at the backwards R. "I hate to say it, Jerry, but your work stinks."

"Don't fall prey to the idiot machine."

"I'm tired of your shit."

"Please try to understand...understand that there is something beneath what is floating on the surface...some profound truth. Perhaps this whole experience is challenging us to reach into the infinite."

"Into the infinite? C'mon! The only thing about it that's infinite is its stench."

"Well, I'm beginning to think that you're stupidity is also infinite."

During the succeeding three days, the chasm that parted our aesthetic sensibilities widened significantly. However, I had also emitted and, through an acute awareness of geometrical variations and a knowledge of the distortion and violence apparent in varying shades, interpreted three more letters. The first consisted of one elongated line, which could have been interpreted as an I. Instead, I determined that it was actually a one, which inevitably led me to the first letter of the alphabet.

The next expulsion was so profuse that it smothered the surface like algae. After photographing the work and hanging it in my study, I contemplated it for two hours. I was struggling to unveil, struggling to see. See. That was it. Clearly, the next letter I was seeking was a C.

A murky contortion of splotches and fragments submerged in strident browns and smears of raw black formed the next letter. I spent the remainder of that night studying the implications of this furious conglomeration, and finally, I discovered that is was not so much about what was there, but more about what was not there. I had my word: "abstract."

I was studying my latest creation, when she interrupted me by jiggling the doorknob. "Jerry, what are you doing in there? Why is this locked?"

"Please, love. I'll be out in a minute. Patience is a tree with bitter roots, but sweet fruits. I'm merely—"

"Patience is the virtue of asses."

"I'm merely enjoying the latest of my works."

"What letter is it this time?"

I flushed.

The next night, I went beyond the finite; the work I produced transcended time. She pounded on the door. "C'mon! You've been in there two hours!"

I took a sip of my cocktail, then allowed her to enter. "My sincerest apologies."

"There's no letter in there. It's just a bunch of slop."

"You need to spend at least two hours with this piece. Then you will unveil its meaning."

"You want me to stare at your shit for two hours?"

"You're thinking too mainstream," I said. "You're only looking at what's on the surface. Try looking beyond that. Don't you see? This is not about a specific thing that is painted there. It's about a mood that it evokes."

"What? You're nuts."

"This is an emotional conquest. This is art...art that is to be enjoyed solely by me. It is not meant for any market; it is meant for me. I am elite."

"You're nuts. That's not art. That's a pile of crap."

"You're a fool," I said. "Does everything have to be dumbed down for you? It is art because I say that it is art! I am the emissary in darkness. Why don't you join the rest of the idiotic masses with your immediacy?"

I thought I knew, but now I am miserable. She has gone, and I am alone. Every day, I look into the toilet and strive to unscramble what occurred. One thought dominates: abstract art is shit, and shit is abstract art.

Private Collection

B.M. Long

RAINER WAS A patient man, and his back did not hurt. For these reasons, he got the job. For seven hours, five days a week, he would stride across the Silversmithery museum as the guardian. He quickly adapted to his new functions. Wandering from room to room, he envisioned the pieces in their original context. What gracious wrist had held this narrow bracelet? What exquisite wine had this chalice carried? The guardian also checked the visitors, and nodded when they glanced at him. Sometimes, he visited his colleagues from the ticket office or the locker room; or he carried on to the shop.

When Rainier left the Silversmithery team, ten years had gone by. Now, he would look after the Fine Arts museum. What a true blessing, after all this time spent among cups, crowns, and tools! Instead of being produced by his imagination, the scenes materialized under his nose. He interpreted them as he liked. One morning, three characters sitting next to a canoe were fishing; the following day, they were deciding which one of them would not step back on board. Other times, they discussed how to address the individuals at the back of the painting. Rainier even enjoyed naming the cast.

And if his life had been less austere? Would he have loved his job as much? He did not go out much and possessed no friend. Used to not speaking during the day, he was so talkative in the evening that he bored his interlocutors. His universe was almost exclusively limited to his work, and he had trouble varying conversation topics.

One night when he was particularly lonely, he considered that others probably felt the same way. So sprang the idea. Why wouldn't they retail reproductions of the best canvases, at the shop? What a consolation, to offer oneself such nurturing company! Of course, it was already possible to get postcards and posters, but these did not transmit the warmth or the subtlety of the original art. They hadn't the shimmering feeling of life that emerged from the paintings.

The director was receptive. He selected three paintings among the institution's favorites: an aquatic landscape by Claude Monet; a scene populated by tiny figures, depicted by Brueghel the Elder; and a humble snowy house from Octave Bélanger, his favored piece. There were many companies that specialized in reproducing art. The director selected one of them and placed an order. The canvases were attentively rendered in a Chinese workshop. They proved to be sumptuous, strikingly resembling the originals, even up to the frames.

They never sold. Too modest, the city owning the museum did not have enough customers willing to pay the necessary amount for such good reproductions. People kept buying the postcards and posters. Years became decades. Rainier asked to be transferred to the shop, as his legs hurt.

Finally, the loyal employee's career came to an end. As a going away present, the director gave the reproductions. Rainier expressed an odd request: he wished to occupy one last time every role he had played during the past years. Indeed, on several occasions, he had replaced the locker room attendant or the night guard. It was granted with a patronizing smile.

The last day, Rainier greeted his colleagues and put away the carefully wrapped canvases in his car. He arranged the Bélanger in his bedroom and the Monet on top of the sofa. He kept the place of honor for Brueghel the Elder, in the entrance, because that was the direction of his gaze during his meal. In a sublime manner, the paintings transformed the humble apartment. Rainier experienced much happiness from them; without any doubt, it was the crowning achievement of his career. The ex-guardian completed his life as quietly as he had lived it and died shortly after his retirement, as happens sometimes to those who no more have a daily aim.

During the yearly heavy maintenance, the restorers unhooked all the paintings. They studied them meticulously, paying attention to the tiniest sign of wear, administering minuscule adjustments here and there. When they noticed that three pieces wore *Made in China* labels on their reverse, it was already too late. The Salvation Army had cleaned out Rainier's apartment, and the paintings had gone rapidly, because the price asked was extremely low, and because they had the unrivaled radiance of authentic pieces.

Lovebird

Tim Jeffreys

PILAR HAD ONE of the most beautiful gardens in the entire region. There was nothing she enjoyed more than walking there alone: tending her roses, watering gladioli, raking up weeds. She went to her garden sometimes at night, to stare at the moon and stars, to feel the flowers lilting to and fro in the breeze all around. Just being there she felt comforted.

There were always birds in the garden. Inquisitive robins would appear whenever she raked the earth to plant something new. Blackbirds stalked the paved path, looking for snails to snatch from their shells and gobble up. And there was always a thrush or two chirruping in the trees. Pilar loved to hear birdsong, especially in the morning when she would open her bedroom window and lie in bed and listen. She liked to imagine that the birds enjoyed her garden as much as she did. The high stone walls kept foxes out, and she had purposefully planted lavender to deter any feline threats. She had aimed to create a sanctuary in her garden for the birds, in the hope that they would come and sing so she could listen to them.

One fine morning she was out amongst the flowers when, out of the cherry tree at the bottom of the garden, she heard the most extraordinarily beautiful birdsong. She looked up, stunned. Perched on one of the cherry tree's branches was a bird like none she had ever seen. He, for it was immediately apparent to Pilar that it was a he, was the size of a thrush but instead of the brown speckled plumage of that bird he had the most striking yellow and blue feathers. When he sang he would tilt his head back and thrust out his chest, as though in the midst of a most important duty, releasing his song with such authority that it was as if he were compelling the entire world to listen.

"Why, you are a proud one," Pilar said, laughing and gazing up at the bird in wonder.

The bird looked at her, tilting his head to and fro, scrutinizing her with his tiny black eyes. Then he launched into a short bout of victorious song that so surprised and delighted Pilar she gasped with awe. With a flutter then he was gone, darting over the gardens and rooftops, taking his wonderful music with him.

Pilar did not expect to see him again, so she was surprised the next day when she lay in bed listening to the birds, to hear his unmistakable voice cut through all the other song.

"Oh!"

She went to the window and looked out on the garden. The yellow and blue bird was there in the same spot as the previous day, standing out against the leaves of the cherry tree. He lifted his head as though he saw her and launched his song at her window. Pilar laughed with joy and clapped her hands.

So it went. The beautiful bird returned every day to the cherry tree in Pilar's garden and would sing, so she liked to think, especially for her. She was a rapt and attentive audience. Sometimes she brought out a lounger and would lie in the sun, half-drowsy with pleasure, as the little bird sang. As more days passed, Pilar became aware of the approach of autumn. She felt it growing steadily colder. She knew that most of the birds in her garden would take flight for the winter. When, one day, the little yellow and blue bird failed to make an appearance in her garden, she felt a terrible pain in her heart. She had taken such joy in the bird's singing that without it nothing could please her. She walked the garden with a heavy heart. Now that there was frost in the morning, some of the flowers were drooping and dying. The cherry tree was shedding its leaves. Soon it would be nothing but a skeleton of twisted branches. Seeing this, Pilar could only sigh.

The following morning when she woke, her heart leapt when she heard the familiar trill of the yellow and blue bird. Jumping out of bed, she went to the window. There the bird was, on his favourite branch of the cherry tree, singing his little heart out. Pilar laughed out loud to see him.

But then she thought: *How can I stop him from leaving for good? I don't think I can face the winter without him. How can I get him to stay here with me, for good, so I can listen to his singing every day and feel happy?*

She had an idea. That day she went to the market and bought an expensive, ornate birdcage.

It doesn't matter the cost, she thought. *Not when it's for him – my little yellow and blue friend. He deserves only the best.*

When she arrived home she hung the birdcage by the window in her kitchen. Standing back, she thought how attractive it looked hanging there. It would be more attractive still with the colourful little songbird occupying it.

The next morning when she heard the bird singing, she put on her slippers and, taking some bread, went out in her nightdress to the garden. The yellow and blue bird was on his usual perch on the cherry tree. Pilar began breaking pieces of the bread and tossing it into the grass.

“Here little birdie,” she said. “The ground’s too hard to dig for worms now. Have some bread. Here. Come on.”

The little bird fell silent and watched her, turning his head from side to side.

Pilar continued to encourage him. “Come on, little birdie. It’s okay. Nothing can harm you in my garden. You’re quite safe. Come on.”

At last the bird gave a chirrup and dived for a piece of bread. Pilar laughed. She began to move backwards, leaving a trail of bread for the bird. He hopped along the path, eating up the crumbs. Pilar soon felt the kitchen door at her back. She enticed the bird inside. He seemed wary at first, but at Pilar’s gentle coaxing he hopped inside and about the tiles. Making sure she had his attention, Pilar placed the last piece of bread inside the birdcage. The bird stood still and eyed the cage.

“Go on. Don’t you want it? Go on.”

The bird gave her a glance. Then he fluttered up and through the door of the cage. Pilar gently closed the cage door once he was inside.

Now he’s trapped, she thought. She felt an immediate pang of guilt, but then the bird began singing so merrily that her guilt vanished and she clapped her hands together, laughing.

“Oh you vain little thing!” she said. “You’re happy now you’ve found an audience, aren’t you? I know what kind of bird you are now, little man! A lovebird! You know I love you, don’t you! You’re happy being here with me too, aren’t you! ”

This was what she told herself, but as the days passed, though the bird still sang for her every morning, puffing out his little chest, he would spend the rest of the day huddled on his perch, silent and gazing toward the window. He was such a sorry sight that Pilar could not bear it. She went to the window and opened it as wide as she could. She could not stop herself shredding a few tears as she then went to open the door on the cage.

“I’m sorry I made you a prisoner,” she said. “Go on and fly away. Fly south for the winter or whatever it is you do when it gets too cold here. Go on now, you weren’t meant to be in a cage little one.”

The bird did not move. It only gazed at her.

“Go on,” she said again. “You know I love you, but you can’t stay caged up forever. Fly, fly.”

But he would not fly.

Pilar went to lie down for a while, leaving the window and the cage door open. She expected, when she returned, that the bird would be gone. In the end she fell asleep, and stayed in bed longer than she intended.

When she woke, she dashed downstairs and into the kitchen, certain that the bird would have gone, but he was right there in his cage. When he saw Pilar he began to sing. She could not help but feel happy.

"But what are you doing?" she cried. "You're breaking my heart. Why won't you fly away?"

From then on Pilar left the door of the cage open. Every morning when she woke, the bird would puff out his chest and sing for her, and she would always smile. She would open the window wide incase this happened to be the day that the little bird chose to fly away. But the bird did not seem to want to go. He would spend the day huddled on his perch, like always, and Pilar would feel so sad seeing him that she began to feel resentful.

"Your cage is open, why don't you go!" she found herself yelling at the bird one day. "I'm not stopping you. Go, go – if that's what you want! Don't sit there looking pitiful – go!"

He would not go. Pilar began to hate him for it. Now in the mornings when she woke and he started to sing she would became raked with guilt and yell at him to be quiet. She cursed the day he had first flown down and perched on the branches of her cherry tree.

How the Howling Darkness Finds Me

F. Charles Murdock

I DON'T REMEMBER how I learned of the Fields of Becoming, that nowhere-place where a special few can trade themselves for another, by parts or in whole. I know I'd searched for its elusive door for most my life, though, and had sacrificed much and many along the way. And now, in my sixty-fifth year, I believe I've finally found the path to the Fields and an escape from this Forgetting.

Now all I have to do is wait for them to leave, those people who whisper and stare, those strangers who say I should know them. They call themselves my loved ones but linger like nightmares, always asking how I feel. They feed me and keep me clean. Some of them weep and hold my withered hands to their hearts, but I endure their pity because my escape is nigh.

Before I lost my voice and then so much more, I'd asked those strangers for a mirror, telling them I wanted to remember who I once was. Despite the odd request, they'd obliged and soon a large looking glass was placed at the side of my bed just inches from my face.

I looked then and probed and peered, staring into the reflected void with an open heart. And when the void stared back, I stood my ground. I met the blackness with an unblinking eye and so was rewarded for my patience and courage when the doorway revealed itself like a secret scar.

Now comes the late hour when the strangers leave me to sleep and I turn to the mirror one last time. In its surface I see well the wraith this disease has created. For a time I was ashamed of the gnarled thing staring back at me, but soon realized that accepting the reflection was the only way to escape, that beyond it was the Fields of Becoming where all wrongs could be undone.

I stare into the glazed eyes of the old man in the glass, engaging him in a contest of silent riddles. I approach him, slowly at first, but then with confidence and growing zeal. A moment later I'm out of my body and into his for he is the keeper of the doorway.

I leap in a great arc like lightning across the prongs of a Jacob's ladder, the thick blackness of his pupils a deep tunnel that swells around me until it devours the world I once knew. I see the shimmering gateway then and already I've begun to forget the Forgetting.

I follow the gleam of the door through the lurching darkness. As I approach the light I hear the screams of lost souls. My heart goes out to them, but I push past, not wanting to sacrifice salvation for pity.

When I arrive at the gilded threshold, I am bathed in golden light and the great door creaks open because it understands... it knows how long I've reached out for it through the void and just how much I've given to pass beyond.

"All these years," I whisper. "It's finally over."

So the door draws me in, swallows me whole, and at last I'm there and know all will be set right.

In the Fields of Becoming grow not blossoms and fruit but limbs and torsos, faces and skin. Organs thrumming with life are buried in the ashen soil atop arterial roots. And now beneath a hazy, golden sky I look out upon these rolling fields of flesh and bone and weep, knowing in my heart I will survive the tragedy that befell me on the other side of the door.

I search with eye and hand, sifting through this province of dismemberment to find the parts that will match my dying body. Slowly I collect pieces to make me better, breaking off my limbs and stripping away skin, swapping them out to become healthy and new.

Thus in my wake I leave a trail of who I was. Here a tooth, there a kidney... I am shadowed by a row of gore. This is how the howling darkness finds me at the heart of the Fields of Becoming.

I hear the screams beyond the fruit of the Fields, can sense the wall of jealous darkness approaching from behind. The hazy atmosphere groans and totters, the ground begins to quake. All the while the void crawls toward me, shambling along my trail like some dying creature, speaking my name with the voices of those just beyond my dim recollection.

So the blackness slithers on, the very same that possessed the beguiling eyes of my reflection, its screech forcing me to my knees. With effort I crane my head to the folding horizon and see all the figures I once knew.

The darkness swallows the garden, eclipsing the harvest, each body part squealing as its root is lost to the void. I can hear them out there, those who I loved and loved me too, those still alive beyond the Forgetting. They've come in a black fog to take me back. As the garden's many streams of blood curdle and rot, I realize my coming is too late.

There had only been time enough for a glimpse of this place, for but a waning sliver of hope in my old heart. The Fields of Becoming will itself become a void of undoing. And thus I lose myself again. Despite my courage I become just another aimless screamer in the void, a prisoner of my dearest memories.

"All those years," I whisper as the darkness pulls me to pieces, these writhing seeds planting themselves in this purgatorial garden for the next fool to purchase with his soul.

"It's finally over," I say with a mouth that falls to pieces.

And then there is only the darkness and I no longer forget. The memories I'd lost are still there, buried in the hungry void, coming in flashes I cannot fully grasp. I am forever lost to the world though I've reclaimed these memories, all of which I will never again be able to share with those I love.

So I have become another frail phantom who let the door snap shut behind him. And I have to wonder if they are still out there, those strangers who I loved and who loved me, those from my reclaimed memories.

I wonder if they hear me screaming from the void.

Right Train, Wrong Destination

S.P. Lazarus

ON A SWELTERING summer afternoon in 1979 I found myself sitting sandwiched between two sweat-smelling ruffians in a crowded train—an anachronism burning coal and spewing acrid black smoke—that left Tatanagar Station as if it never intended to reach any specific destination; it crawled; it stopped at every wayside station; and it even made door-deliveries of passengers at any place of their convenience, which they indicated by pulling the chain.

In my lap was a plate of food, which (as hungry as I was) I hesitated to refer to by that name. On the plate was a regular railway assortment: a few chapattis, some dhal, an odd looking curry, a little curd and some rice. But it was now difficult to separate one dish from the other since they had run into one another—blame that on callous handling—and was now an unattractive mush. And as I continued to curse and stare at it, my appetite began to diminish and my aversion reached a point where fasting was preferable to eating this mess.

But when I looked up from my plate I saw many eyes staring, staring not at me, but at my plate. Not with the disgust with which I perceived it, but as a meal. Some pairs of eyes looked at the plate furtively. Those pairs of eyes belonged to grown-ups. But some pairs of eyes were staring at it with the longing of a man in the middle of a desert for whom water—any quality of water—would be life-saving nectar. Those pairs of eyes belonged to children. And there were half a dozen of them—ages ranging from about two to about sixteen. Their minds were busy as they imagined savouring the contents of my plate. Their mouths were salivating with anticipation. A faint streak of drool dribbled down the side of their respective chins.

Their mother sat motionless, her gaze fixed on some imaginary object of interest on the floor of the compartment, the bottom of her saree was riding well above her knees on which she rested her arms and her patched threadbare pallu was coiled around her neck. Their father looked pickled. A half smoked beedi hung limply from his lips. His gaze seemed to be fixed on the wisps of smoke that wafted away from him. And what was there for him to look forward to?

The four boys—all but the youngest shirtless—sat open-mouthed, the corners of which showed clear signs of scurvy. All wore a chain of faded black string knotted evenly throughout its length clearly indicating that they were objects of religious significance. Their hair originally black had turned to a shade of dirty brown due to lack of care and prolonged exposure to direct sunlight. Their faces were filthy and a couple of them had traces of dried snot around their nostrils. All of them had a singular focus: my plate.

The eldest and youngest of the siblings were girls. The eldest was about sixteen. She wore a skirt and blouse. Like her mother she too let her skirt ride above her knees. Both the skirt and blouse were in a state of neglect: they were torn; torn and patched; and direly needed replacing. In her lap was the youngest—not more than two years; tears welled in her eyes and the snot was beginning to peek out of her nostrils as she hesitantly asked her sister for the contents of my plate. The elder girl held the younger one close to her bosom with one hand and stroked her hair with the other trying to take the child's mind away from food.

This was an adivasi (tribal) family. The adivasis of Orissa were from the Keshapur area; they were landless; they were illiterate; they were poor; and their life at the best of times was miserable. Most often women were the worse sufferers. They were discriminated against. They were the victims of violence. Some were killed on suspicion of practicing witchcraft. Young girls were thought of as a burden by their own families and sometimes sold off for prices ranging from 40 to 2000 rupees. The poor here were only getting poorer.

An imperfect god. An imperfect world. So much disparity. The haves have so much and many have-nots not even food. God does everything for the best they say—even when he starves children. Try telling that to these children. Illiterate they may be, but nothing could be more ludicrous even to them.

My conscience was kicking my butt: a mere moment ago I had dismissed the pile on my plate as crap and yet here were half a dozen mouths so hungry that they would have gratefully shared it among themselves.

"You want?" I asked instinctively in both words and gestures. The older among the children hesitated. The younger ones nodded instantly as their hands spontaneously reached for my plate.

I batted an eyelid. The plate was clean. But hunger was as apparent on these disappointed little faces as was surprise on mine. I was helpless. All I could do was stare at these poor children who by years of deprivation and disappointment were conditioned to accept situations such as these. They quickly reconciled to the fact that even a morsel was better than outright starvation—this was all they were getting in the foreseeable future.

A few minutes later the train came to a halt at a place that was only a little better than a sand heap and a small shed with a moss covered asbestos roof which was the station master's cabin—beats standing under a tree. It was a station and it was a scheduled stop. There was frenzied scurrying as people tried to get on as others tried to get off—at the same time. And pushing his way in was the lunch man to collect the empty plates.

"Can you give me some more lunch," I asked.

"No lunch," he said. "Plate collection," he added as much as to explain the reason for the train's stoppage.

Another proof that this train was an antiquated museum piece was that every time it halted all the fans and lights ceased to work. This only served to exacerbate my torture: a crowded compartment, a bursting bladder, the heat searing through the train's metal roof and a still summer afternoon when the ambient temperature was in the region of 110. And I dared not get up from my seat for fear of losing it. However, just when it all seemed so hopeless, the old wreck began to move. What a relief!

As the train chugged along at a leisurely walking pace, I saw women in sarees that covered the area just above the knees and just below their sensuously flabby paunch. Almost all of them carried a bundle of long poles—they weren't bamboo for sure, but something equally pliable. And as the women walked lugging their burden, the bundle of poles bobbed up and down in rhythm with the wiggling of their firm bottoms and the jingling of their ample bosoms that were more exposed than covered. That was a sight. But to anyone familiar with this part of the world it was routine.

Then running along the tracks were vendors who quite easily hopped onto the slow-moving train. They carried little baskets with roasted peanuts or cucumber—delicacies under different circumstances. Today's journey was probably the worst train journey of my life. But there were other times—memorable times—when the journey -in spite of almost 36 hours in a clammy compartment—was pleasant. Friends. Chatting. Smoking. Sometimes splitting beers. It almost equalled the pleasure of going home after a long time away. In fact as much as I longed to get home as soon as I could, I hated it when the journey ended. But today I ignored the vendors even though they literally stuck their wares in my face. But there were others looking at the vendors' baskets with childish longing. It was impossible not to notice the cumulative yearning of the six starving children.

I decided to be liberal. After all it wasn't my money. But that's another story. I'll come to that soon. Hunger expresses itself in a language that is universally understood. I could see hungry eyes follow the peanut vendor.

"Hello," I called the peanut man.

"A packet for each of the children," I said in English and gestured using the simplest sign language.

Something the man replied in Oriya made the two sweat stinking heavyweights on either side of me giggle.

The man made paper cones with deftness that comes only with practice. And into each he poured a small tin can of peanuts and handed them to the eager outstretched hands. When his job was done, he collected his money and when he was sure he wasn't going to get any more business from this compartment, he jumped off the slow-moving train ran along the track for just a few seconds before climbing into the next bogey. As if this was the cue that the cucumber man was waiting he soon replaced the peanut man.

"You want?" I asked the children tilting my head in the direction of the new vendor. There was a chorus of nodding heads.

The cucumbers were already skinned. The cucumber man picked up each piece, made hurried slits on its side and gave each a generous sprinkling of chilly powder and salt before handing them to the children. He did all this with lightning speed. To him time was money. He had to cover as many compartments as he could before he reached the next station from where he would take the down train to return home.

Where the children possibly saw a saviour in me, the vendor saw a sucker and decided to make the best of the situation. He gave each of the children as many cucumbers as they could hold. I did not mind. Like I said before, it was after all not my money.

Again the overgrown stinkers by my side said something and giggled. While I was arguing more in favour of ignoring what I presumed were taunts in an alien language rather than take umbrage, the fellow on my left patted me on my back in an obvious gesture of appreciation of what I was doing. And before I knew it, he got up from his seat by the window and offered to trade places with me. And when I appreciatively declined he insisted. When I realized that these two hulks—although they appeared to be ruffians were in fact not—I asked them with signs and a sprinkling of words if I could go to the toilet and if they would keep my seat. They laughed as they nodded. I took that as an affirmation.

There were people sitting everywhere. The compartment was in fact more crowded than I realized. There were people sitting on the luggage racks. They sat in the space between facing seats and they sat in the aisles. Getting to the toilet was a feat. Using it after reaching it was an achievement. It was filthy beyond description. But not having gone to the toilet in more than twelve hours, I simply had to go. And if I did not make use of this opportunity, I did not know if I would get another opportunity before reaching my destination, not knowing where my benevolent hulks were going. I tiptoed around the crap, covered my mouth and nose and took a leak while trying to maintain my balance and at the same time trying not to breathe.

This was without doubt the worst train journey of my life: a wooden plank for a seat, crushed between two stinking mountains of flesh, no proper food, no sleep and not even the luxury of taking a peaceful leak in a clean toilet.

Getting back to my seat was hell and back. But thankfully, true to their word the hulks had prevented anyone from occupying my seat. The moment I sat down I knew that there had been some rearrangement in the seating of the adivasis. The oldest of the siblings had handed the youngest to their mother who was nursing her. The woman did not bother to cover herself. And to most of my suburban co-passengers this did not seem odd. But I was different from them. I was young, college educated, a city dweller with a more than the average libido: that was titillating.

Every time I looked away from the woman my eyes rested on her daughter —the eldest of the siblings. I saw that she was dirty—no *filthy*—hair knotted, dirty finger nails, bedraggled clothes torn in more places than they were stitched. And yet beneath the filth and grime was a pristinely beautiful tribal belle—undeniably. I couldn't help staring at her. Like a scanner I took in her image from head to toe.

Think what a thorough washing and a professional makeover could do. It would be a dramatic transformation. I thought of many of Bollywood's heartthrobs who wore so much makeup—layer upon layer—that if someone should slap them it will fall off their face like a mask.

Without their makeup they would pale in comparison to this dark-eyed beauty.

As I continued to look at her I wondered if she knew that she was beautiful. I couldn't think of any other woman who looked as beautiful as her without even being aware of her good looks and without even trying to look beautiful. And then suddenly I realized that I was brazenly staring at an innocent young tribal girl. I quickly turned away.

And when I did, I noticed both her father and mother looking at me. Surprisingly both were appreciative of my appreciation of their daughter. I could glean that much from their approving smile. And then the man said something in Oriya. The two hooligans by my side made a few rapid comments and the three men giggled.

Then one of the hulks turned to me and asked: "Like?"

"What?" I responded feigning ignorance of what he was so obviously referring to.

The hulk's head tilted to one side and he pointed to the girl with his eyes as his lips broke into an impish smile.

"What are you talking about?" I asked.

You know damn well what I am talking about, said his naughty grin.

For some time at least I resisted the temptation of looking at the young girl. I looked out of the window. There was not much to see: no flora, no fauna, just vast undulating stretches of emptiness, hillocks to the fore and mountains in the distance. Vapour rose up like myriad spirits released from hell rising up to the heavens as the scorching sun sucked up the remaining moisture from the last season's sparse rain. The heat, lack of sleep and the slow rhythmic chugging of the train lulled me to sleep. I don't know for how long I slept but when I woke up I could see from the azure flecks in the far away west that the sun had just set and that the train had come to a halt.

There was a flurry of vendors running on the pavement trying to sell a variety of their wares in the brief time that the train halted. I bought a veritable smorgasbord of victuals not caring how much it cost—and trust me, no matter what I bought it cost me a mere pittance—everything in this part of the world cost no more than a few Rupees. Come on, you can do better than that, I mocked each vendor that came along; Ram Babu will feel insulted if he ever came to know that I fed a family of adivasis at a mere pittance. Ram Babu was the chairman of my company—God bless the saintly man. Everyone—and not just the employees' of his numerous companies—readily agreed that he was indeed a saintly man—not only because he reimbursed our on-duty expenses; paid his employees generously; money was the least of his interests. What he made—and he made many a ton—was incidental or perhaps the fruits of the ingenuity of his forefathers.

When the commotion died down and my mind was beginning to go blank it subconsciously latched onto a subject of interest: the young tribal girl. As the minutes ticked by my obsession with the girl became more brazen. My gaze was riveted to her, oblivious of the fact that the compartment was crowded and that there were people watching me; the girl's parents were watching me and so too the two hulks by my side.

Every now and then the girl's blurry-eyed father said something to her mother. And every time the stony faced woman said nothing. She continued to stare at her imaginary lodestone. The man then said something to the hulks sitting by my side. Both nodded after a pensive moment. I knew that I was the topic of their discussion even though they conversed in Oriya—a language I did not understand—because they kept looking at me as they spoke.

Intermittently their conversation came to halt and a question was addressed to me. I merely stared at them—a quizzical look on my face—not knowing a word of what they were asking. And yet they waited for an answer. Some nerve.

More nerve. They stared back at me waiting for my reply. The hulks even made signs for me to say something. I felt so compelled that I either nodded or shook my head without knowing how pertinent or absurd I was. Sometimes my response elicited a disapproving glare. Sometimes it was a nod of approval. I was totally lost.

Fortunately the train pulled into a station that had the semblance of a regular station. There was a station master's cabin, a few food and sundry stalls on the platform and most important the station itself was lit. However as expected the lights went out and the fans stopped when the train came to a halt. Nevertheless this came as welcome respite: it stopped the unintelligible banter.

It also happened that this was the last watering hole for the night: even though the train was destined to halt at numerous more stations, this would be the last station where food and water would be available. As expected the dinner man came to the window taking dinner orders.

Even though the inside of the compartment was dark I could still make out eight hungry faces. I knew that asking them if they wanted dinner was superfluous; I took the liberty of ordering food for the adivasi family and myself and for the first time for the hulks by my side. All of them accepted their food gratefully. I ate my own dinner with less difficulty: in the semidarkness of the compartment I couldn't see what I was eating. Besides I was hungry.

After about half an hour the train pulled out. The lights came back on and the fans resumed spewing warm air that it sucked in from the still hot roof. With nothing else to do conversations resumed everywhere. The evening wore on; the heat of the afternoon began to lessen; a cool breeze began to blow in through the windows on one side and out the opposite side. People began to unravel sleeping bundles occupying every inch of available space. Lights were turned off, save the solitary blue light that made the difference between total darkness and faint visibility. Conversations gave way to snoring. I kept staring out through the window hoping to see some wayside hamlet. But nothing. Not even a distant light to indicate that there was life out there somewhere.

Sheer boredom must have lulled me to sleep. When I became vaguely aware of my bearings it was early morning. The sun was up and so too people who were to alight at the station that was approaching. It must have been a station of relative importance. Even before the train reached the station there was a handful of buildings—huts first and then brick and mortar—on both sides of the track. And then the station itself—Waltair Railway Station—I was halfway home.

I was still bleary-eyed when I felt a tap on my shoulder: it was one of the hulks saying goodbye. Then my focus shifted to the still partially dark inside of the compartment. I noticed that half the crowd had emptied. And then sitting on the floor close to my feet I saw something that shook me out of my daze. It was the young adivasi girl. When I realized that neither her parents nor her siblings were anywhere there I knew that something awful had happened.

I turned to the hulk. He read the question on my horrified face. With a mixture of Telugu, Oriya and sign language he explained to me that the girl's parents had left her to my care.

"But why should I take care of her? Where are her parents?"

"Brahampur. Brahampur," he said gesturing that they had alighted at that station.

"Why did they leave this girl behind?" I asked puzzled and worried.

Again using combo-communication the hulk made me understand that that is what I had agreed to.

I agreed to no such thing. How ludicrous.

I was furious. My eyes ached with the sudden rush of blood to my head. I felt an agonizing pounding at the temples. How could they do this to me?

This was too high a price the parents expected me to pay for my esthetic appreciation of their daughter's unspoiled beauty.

The least they could have done before saddling me with such an unreasonable responsibility was to have taken my consent.

What do I do now? I began to weigh my options: the worst from my perspective—take the girl home with me; the worst from the girl's perspective—just leave her here; and then the middle course—give her enough money for her to get back home.

As I weighed the three options, the other hulk that had carried their luggage off the train came and stood outside leaning against the bars of the window. Between the two of them they made me understand that the girl's parents were in fact taking her to Brahampur to sell her to a fifty year old man for Rs. 200. Realizing that their daughter's life would be hell after that, they decided that she would have a better life with me even if only as my domestic help.

"Whatever may have been their reason how can I take this girl home with me?" I held the hand of the hulk closest to me and pleaded. "I can't take her with me. I can't take her with me. Help me. Help me... Please." I kept begging.

Bloody hulks...They were a part of this scheme...They knew that this was what the parents had planned... Can you take her with you? I'll give you money—"

"Sorry," said the man nearest to me and pulling his hand away from mine turned and began to walk away with his companion following him.

"Please... Please..." I yelled to no avail.

Conniving bastards.

I looked heavenward for divine intervention. Nothing.

After staring vacantly at the crowds exiting the station I turned to look at the girl. She just sat there cringing in a corner, her lips twitching involuntarily with fear. I could see desperation and pleading in her eyes. I sat down, my head cradled in my hands, my eyes closed and all my faculties numbed. And then when I looked up—I don't know after how long—the hulks were gone and so too was Waltair Railway Station. But the girl was still there. And the train began to pick up speed.

Christmas

Andrew MacKenzie

TAKES A COUPLE seconds to get a good hold on the hammer, the grip is long gone, fingers raw against the rubber handle. Will the grip tighter and swing at the wall. The head sinks into the rotting plasterboard, erupts with gritty dust. No masks on the first day, PPE not all been delivered yet will be first thing in the morning for definite alright buddy. Until then short small breaths, control the heart rate let the sweat out in the heat, keep calm, steady. Smash again, keep at the stud inside the wall, weaken the supports first and you can rip off big chunks of the shit, send them crashing onto the floor, easier to tidy up later. Stack the big bits under the window for easy dumping into the skip. Soggy plaster grit flies into the eyes again, can't touch them, whole face is covered, will rub more in, just make it worse, keep blinking, eyes open as little as possible to make sure the hammer line's in check, keep the head back as far as you can, not too far, the arm's numb, need to keep close, to hit hard enough to do the job, break the plaster, bend the stud. Back's burning got to shift the feet, change up the swinging motion, heels are screaming though the bone feels mushy like it's caving in. Dust everywhere can't see the other wall now, getting hotter, harder to keep the breathing short. I cough and spit on the plaster at my feet. It's thick and black and burns the throat coming up. Keep blinking, turn the head away from the grit.

"That's break."

I put my hand up to cover the sun, "Break, Sammy?"

He nods and pulls his head out, his mask hanging under his chin. The dust washes around in the sunlight. The sounds of hammering and tearing have faded, can hear the boys shuffling out, dust is already thinning.

"Just give's a minute." I keep hammering, putting the back into it, until the break line reaches the floor. I let the hammer go and try to straighten the fingers but can't yet, give it a minute. Half of a board is hanging off of the wall, lost contact with the screws that were holding it in place, a nudge and it'll tear to the floor, breaking, sending clouds of dust into the air. I walk out to the break unit.

When I return it is still there, half a wall's worth, clinging on by nothing more than habit, its supports ripped out from under it. Hammering and pounding fills the air again. The back and arms are aching, stiffened up over the break, have to get the blood pumping again. Get to work on a fresh wall with the sledge hammer, can guess where the stud is now. Ten minutes and I've got the supports weak enough. The fingers are ringing fiercely, can feel them creak around the claw hammer, machine-like, in need of oil. Back screaming, keep the posture tight, spread the strain. One step at a time. Pause for a few breaths, shallow, keep that shite out of the lungs as much as possible, sour and filthy. Back straight, eyes closed as much as you can.

"That's finishing time."

I look over at him, his black mask hanging from his chin, sweat streaks where it clung to his face. The rest of the boys are moving out behind him, faces as dirty as mine. The room is done, mostly, except for the half wall, hanging on by nothing but habit.

"Aye, Sammy."

He pulls his head out. I let the hammer drop onto the rubble and walk after him, past the half wall. The house is silent, except for the boys' boots on the stairs. I leave it hanging.

"We'll get the rest of that PPE in tomorrow lads, sorry about today."

I stretch out on the mattress and moan as the back lets go, everything ringing, can hear it, almost, the muscles ringing, sort of filling up the head. The house is silent, completely still. I rub the palms together, listening to the dry skin sand itself, the tiny skin flakes float into the air, swim around in the lamp light.

"We've got those masks and gloves in."

"Cheers Sammy."

The half wall is still there, sagging now, close to falling under its own weight. Banging and scraping begin to fill the air. I tighten the mask over the face, the elastic wraps dig around the ears, and get into the rubble with the shovel, moving over to the window for easy loading into the skip. Stay low, no point in fully straightening up between loads, bigger distance for the back to cover. Dig into the big stacks, then brush the debris back together, repeat. Dust is so thick can't see the wall in front, the sun making a fog out of the grey shite. Mask is clogged up already, tough to suck in enough air, like I need one of those nose tubes hooked up to an air supply, like my lungs are too weak to breathe by themselves, anymore, skin sagging to old plasterboard yellow, arms too wasted to lift. I grab onto the wheelie bin and work it over to the window, tip the broken board and compacted dust into the skip.

"That's break."

I turn around as a shape backs away into the dust.

"Aye, Sammy."

Don't usually read a paper during the break, quiet enough to read just fine mind you, just rustling and the occasional cough or attempt to blow some of the dust out of the nose from the lads but here's an unattended one and it's quieter than usual being a weekend shift. Can't quite keep the eyes focused on the words mind you, it's quiet too quiet, Christ a bit of rain even would do the trick but another boiler today. Five minutes in I give it up and drop it on its front. Local amateur team is doing well and posing for a team photo on the back cover, must be around fifteen at the oldest. Same age as the boy would be. Christ it's quiet though.

I move into the room with the double layer over the chipboard, ahead of the rest of them. Can't just swing at this one, can't go into without a plan so to speak, will be here till next week trying to bash this one down, so I knock about a bit until I find where the stud is, measure it out around the room and up the ladder and into the attic on the other side, going at the stud with the sledge from the top. Once I start to separate it from the ceiling some light comes through. Can see a black bag, Christmas tinsel spilling out of it. I stop to catch the breath some, air's thick and old in here, and pull the bag over with the hammer. Cards fall out of it and I pick up a yellowed one gone wavy with age and hold it up to the crack, signed by Agnes and Sandy next door and underneath Calum age 8 in perhaps crayon and I throw it far into the attic so the light can't reach it, along with the rest of the old shite, and the noise is muffled up here got to get back down fuck it I'll get the wall down in my own time.

About the Contributors

Sana Aslam

Sana Aslam is a Creative Writing MA student at Nottingham Trent University. Her work has been published in the anthology 'Moths at the Bus Stop' (Launderette Books, 2013), which she co-edited and designed. She is interested in classic fairy tales and magic realism of the Angela Carter variety. You can follow her on twitter @Sana_Lewis

Sally Barnett

Sally Barnett is an Illustrator/Graphic Artist presently studying BA in Graphic Design and Illustration. Her passion is children's book illustration and the fantastical.

Sally was born in Bath and after leaving art college, trained professionally as a Civil Engineer, but gave it all up a few years ago for her first love of Illustration.

She loves walking and photography, has also trained in Pest Control and Arc welding and loves finding new things to try, that doesn't involve heights. Sally can be contacted through her website: www.sallybarnett.co.uk

Carina Bissett

In another life, Carina Bissett wrote travel articles and books about the Southwest. These days, Carina spends her time crafting twisted fairy tales and cross-pollinated mythic fiction. Her short fiction and poetry can be found at the Journal of Mythic Arts, The NonBinary Review and other assorted journals and anthologies. She is currently at work on the first novel in her five-book Elements series.

Matthew Bartlett

Matthew M. Bartlett was born in Hartford, Connecticut in 1970. He lives in Northampton, Massachusetts with his wife Katie and their five cats. His book "Gateways to Abomination" was released in late July 2014 to excellent reviews.

M.R. Cosby

M.R. Cosby writes short, dark fiction—mostly interpreting his own experience, and from his dreams. He tries to find the strangeness in the every day, and to expose the gaps that people unwittingly find themselves slipping through. He has had a lifelong interest in dark literature, which started after being exposed to the Pan collections of horror stories at a tender age. He began writing his memoirs some years ago, which, though still incomplete, provided the inspiration for his first collection of strange stories, Dying Embers.

Martin was the Creative Director of a large publishing firm, working on a varied stable of magazines. During this time he contributed to many features as a journalist and his appetite for writing was thoroughly whetted.

Martin is currently working on his next collection of short stories, organising his family, and thinking about a novel.

George Cromack

George Cromack lives in North Yorkshire, England, and works as a tutor in adult education. 'Cold Calling' a short film scripted by George is currently making its way around the festival circuit. Aside from scripts, he also writes short stories. 'Hooky Pook' is an unpublished story initially inspired by variations on colloquial names for gargoyles.

David Elliott

David Elliott is a writer and musician, originally from Liverpool, UK. His short fiction has been published by a wide variety of magazines, such as Penumbra, The Rusty Nail, 69 Flavors of Paranoia, The Satirist, Danse Macabre, Apocrypha and Abstractions, and Eunoia Review.

James Everington

James Everington is a writer of supernatural fiction whose work has appeared in Supernatural Tales, Morpheus Tales and the Little Visible Delight anthology, amongst others. His second collection of short stories, Falling Over, is out now from Infinity Plus and a monthly serial, The Quarantined City, is due 2015 from Spectral Press.

Oh and he drinks Guinness, if anyone's asking. You can find out what James is currently up to at: http://www.jameseverington.blogspot.co.uk/

Martin Greaves

Martin Greaves worked in menial clerical jobs for many years, toiling under sodium strip lights that gave his skin the deathly pallor of a corpse whilst breathing in the acrid fumes of photocopying toner. Finally, he escaped his bonds to study Illustration at Manchester University and now spends his days skipping gaily through lush meadows of wild flowers and drawing strange pictures that seep into the myriad thought-chambers of his mind.

O.L. Humphreys

Oliver Humphreys grew up in the Royal Forest of Dean, Gloucestershire, an area covered with dense, ancient woodland and heavy with mysticism. He spent most of his childhood in his bedroom playing computer games. He now lives in the much less mystical West London suburb of Ealing with his wife Daniele, and is recovering from an on-line chess addiction.
Oliver began writing short fiction when living in Northampton, where he joined a local science fiction writers group.
His physical appearance could be described as somewhere between quantity surveyor and structural engineer, but with a beard. On the whole he has a placid, easygoing temperament. However is likely to fly into a rage if his cider is served over ice.
To date his only other published short story is 'The Thin Dead Line' in Terror Tree's Pun Book of Horror Stories published by KnightWatch Press.

Tim Jeffreys

Tim Jeffreys is the author of five collections of short stories, the most recent being 'From Elsewhere', aswell of the first two books of his Thief saga. His short fiction has also appeared in various international anthologies and magazines. In his work he incorporates elements of horror, fantasy, absurdist humour, science-fiction and anything else he wants to toss into the pot to create his own brand of weird fiction.
Visit him online at www.timjeffreyswriter.webs.com.

Beau Johnson

Beau Johnson has been published before, mostly on the darker side of town. Such places might include Underground Voices, Shotgun Honey, Out Of The Gutter Online and/or Bartleby Snopes. He lives in Canada with his wife and three young boys, the middle of which is now as bionic as he.

S.P. Lazarus

S.P. Lazarus is the author of two fictions "A Tricycle With Two Wheels" and "An End And A Beginning" and a non-fiction "The Tomb Of Jesus And The Ossuary Of James" for which he is looking for publishers. In the meanwhile he has taken to writing short stories. His stories have appeared in World City Stories, Story Star, Four Quarters, The Reading Hour and Indian Review.

Matthew Lett

Matthew Lett currently lives in Tulsa, OK. with his wife and two daughters. Having written for a number of years, he's the author of several novels, novellas, and short-stories that have appeared both in paperback and e-books. Titles include some of the following: "Woodview Heights: Legacy of Decadence" (3-book series), "He Who Walks the Corridors," "Dead Rain, and "Crimson Snow" to name a few. Matthew enjoys watching football and is a bona-fide horror film fan, and has several other titles due to be published soon.

BM Long

BM Long moved from her native Brussels to Montreal after getting a Master's Degree in Literature. A full-time writer, and part-time library clerk, she has published short stories in several literary magazines. Specializing in meticulous and striking short fiction, her goal is to get the world to read.

Andrew Mackenzie

Andrew Mackenzie is an English Literature student living and writing in Scotland. He founded and runs a creative writing society, and his fiction has appeared in both print and online magazines. When not consuming or writing strange fiction, he boxes and tries to figure out uncomfortable things.

Michael McGlade

Michael McGlade grew up in an Irish farmhouse where the leaky roof didn't bother him as much as the fear of electrocution from the nightly scramble for prime position beneath the chicken lamp, the only source of heating in the house – a large infrared heat lamp more commonly used for poultry. His seminal influences were Darwin's Survival Of The Fattest and a morbid belief that "undying love" meant you had a soft-spot for zombies.

Never allowing these misapprehensions to hold him back from success, he understood that nothing is as clear as the illegible comprehensibility of the modern world. His short fiction has been published in Spinetingler, Dead Harvest, Perihelion, and Amok horror anthology by April Moon Books. He holds a master's degree in English from Queen's University, Ireland. You can find out the latest news and views from him on McGladeWriting.com.

F Charles Murdock

Franklin Charles Murdock is a fiction writer from the Midwestern United States. Though most of his work is harvested from the vast landscapes of horror, fantasy, and science fiction, Franklin strives to spin tales outside the conventions of these genres.

His work has appeared in Dark Fuse, Under the Bed Magazine, 69 Flavors of Paranoia, MicroHorror, Liquid Imagination, Yellow Mama, Heavy Hands Ink, WEIRDYEAR, Phantom Kangaroo, PrimalZine, and various other publications. Most recently, he's been co-authoring the serial epic BEARD THE IMMORTAL on swordandportent.com.

Jeremiah Murphy

From New Jersey to New Mexico to Oklahoma to Nebraska to New York to Indiana to the District of Columbia to Qatar, Jeremiah Murphy--writer, artist, and editor--gets around, leaving broken hearts, clever stories, and scenes of wanton destruction in his wake. Evidence of this can be found at: www.jrmhmurphy.com

Douglas J Ogurek

Douglas J. Ogurek's fiction appears in the British Fantasy Society Journal, The Literary Review, Gone Lawn, Morpheus Tales, and several anthologies. He is the communications manager of a Chicago-based architecture firm, where he has written over 75 articles about facility planning and design. More at www.douglasjogurek.weebly.com.

Michael S Walker

Michael Walker has a BA in English from the Ohio State University. He has seen his poetry, short stories, and criticism published in a number of literary and popular magazines including Weird Tales and The Golden Lantern. His first novel, 7-22 (a young adult fantasy novel) was published by CreativeGuy Publishing in 2013. Currently he lives in Columbus Ohio, where in addition to writing he works on music and art.

Vikki Yeates

Vikki Yeates is an illustrator living and working in Bath, England, although she spent many years in Brighton, where she did a Degree in Illustration in the early 90s.

She would describe her work as 'Gothic Art'; dark, atmospheric images with a dream-like quality, inspired by sinister tales and macabre stories. This type of subject matter is well-suited to her style of drawing, which has been influenced by German Expressionism, particularly the wood-block prints of 'Die Brucke'.

A few years ago she became interested in experimenting with the written word in my paintings, taking the basic idea of illustration one step further, to create works of art which can stand alone. Scratching words into the ink seemed to imbue the picture with power and the words become imagery.

Her black and white work is usually either scraperboard or lino print.

Most of her commercial work these days tends to be wildlife, particularly hares and foxes, but she still tries to make them appear dark and atmospheric. http://vikkiyeates.daportfolio.com